SPY MASTER

FIRST BLOOD

Also by Jan Burchett and Sara Vogler

SPY MASTER

FIRST BLOOD

JAN BURCHETT
& SARA VOGLER

Orion
Children's Books

First published in Great Britain in 2016
by Orion Children's Books
an imprint of Hachette Children's Group
and published by Hodder and Stoughton Limited
Carmelite House
50 Victoria Embankment
London EC4Y 0DZ
An Hachette UK company

1 3 5 7 9 10 8 6 4 2
Copyright © Jan Burchett and Sara Vogler 2016
The right of Jan Burchett and Sara Vogler to be identified
as the authors of this work has been asserted.

A catalogue record for this book is
available from the British Library.

ISBN 978 1 4440 1067 1

Typeset by Input Data Services Ltd, Bridgwater, Somerset

Printed in Great Britain by Clays Ltd, St Ives plc

www.orionchildrensbooks.com

In memory of Auntie Jo,
with grateful thanks for all her support
and encouragement

1

'Goodbye and good riddance, you worthless worm!' Father Busbrig's angry face glared at me through the abbey gates. 'And when you fail – as I'm sure you will – don't come back with your tail between your legs.'

I wanted to reply that it would be difficult to do that as worms don't have legs, but I kept my mouth shut. He'd only waddle out waving his vicious stick, and I was determined to walk away from St Godric's Abbey without a sore bum. He'd thrashed me for the last time.

When I got to the bend in the road, I heard the sound of running feet. I turned, knowing it couldn't be Father Busbrig. The fat old abbot hadn't run for years – not even for the dinner bell. Brother Matthew caught up with me, holding something wrapped in a cloth. I'd already said goodbye to all the monks, but I should have known my godfather wouldn't let me leave without a last word with me alone.

'I forgot to give you this,' he panted, pressing the bundle into my hands. 'Bread for your journey. Don't eat it all at once. Now, do you have the letter safe?'

I nodded, patting my jerkin. 'You've asked me a hundred times. I'm to go straight to Whitehall Palace, shove the letter under King Henry's nose and demand a knighthood on the spot!'

A flash of alarm crossed Brother Matthew's face.

'Or maybe I'll do as you've told me and show it to the Clerk of the Kitchen and he'll give me a job.'

'Then mind you do,' said Brother Matthew, smiling. 'I know your hare-brained schemes.'

'Don't worry,' I told him. 'I won't pester the King straight away.'

I wouldn't be pestering the King at all. I'd be stuck in a steamy kitchen. Every day at the abbey had been the same for as long as I could remember. Prayers, meals, prayers and a lot of hard work in between. I knew that life in the palace kitchen would be exactly the same – without so many prayers!

But it would be a good job and a roof over my head. If I said that to myself enough times, I'd start to believe it.

'Just stay out of trouble,' sighed Brother Matthew.

'I've tried really hard this week,' I replied. 'It wasn't my fault the goat decided to follow me into the chapel and eat the tapestries. It's God's creature and can make up its own mind.'

'And the rotten herring under Father Busbrig's cushion?'

'I had to put it somewhere.'

Brother Matthew chuckled. 'You always have an answer, Jack Briars. Now go. I must get to my prayers. Come and see me when you can. I'll welcome you even if the abbot won't.'

Although he was smiling his eyes were moist. I hoped he wasn't going to cry. That would be too embarrassing, especially as I had a knot in the pit of my stomach and was worried I'd join him if he started. Brother Matthew had been more than a godparent to me, he'd been like a proper father, and I was leaving him for the first time in my life.

'God's speed, Jack.'

I watched him return to the gates, clutching the rough grey wool of his habit to keep it out of the puddles. Then I turned my back on St Godric's. If it hadn't been for Brother Matthew, I'd have been happy never to see it again.

Father Busbrig had always rubbed it in that I was just a foundling and couldn't live on the monks' charity for ever. He said I should be grateful he'd let me live at the abbey at all. And even more grateful that Brother Matthew's cousin worked at Court. According to the miserable old toad, my godfather's letter to William Thynne, the Clerk of the Kitchen, was the only thing keeping me from certain death in a ditch. Although he also informed me that Mister Thynne would take one look at me and slam the door in my face.

I was going to prove him wrong. As much as I didn't yearn to work in the kitchen, I wanted to get the better of fat old Father Busbrig.

The sun was up but the March morning was cold and I strode out to keep warm. I'd not gone far before the bread began to call to me. As I pulled bits off the crust I saw that Brother Matthew had tucked a slice of salted pork in the parcel. An unexpected treat, which was soon gone. It was only after I'd swallowed the last mouthful that I remembered that there'd be no more until I got to Whitehall Palace – seven miles away.

'Coming to join us, Jack?' came a deep voice over the hedge.

Harry Stubbs and his farmhands were at their archery practice.

'I would do,' I called back, grinning, 'but I'd put you all to shame.'

'Aye, you would,' agreed Farmer Stubbs. 'If we were trying to shoot our own feet!'

They laughed. Once, I'd sneaked out of the abbey and they'd let me try shooting a longbow. It was twice as tall as I was and I'd barely been able to pull the string. The arrow had plopped down in front of me.

'Where are you bound for, lad?' asked Seth the cowherd, coming to lean on the gate.

'To see the King,' I said, as if I was a regular visitor at Court. 'Well, to work in his kitchens anyway.'

They wished me luck and I marched on, soon leaving the abbey and Acton Village far behind.

I was starving by the time I could see the church towers of London in the distance. My old boots were chafing my toes. I'd never walked so far in my life. The bells began to chime ten o'clock. It was strange to think that, as I was making my way up the busy road to the cross at Charing, Brother Matthew was on his knees in the abbey chapel. Three hours' walk away and I was in a new world, a world full of English spoken in more strange accents than I'd ever heard. And not only English. A group of horsemen in plumed hats were calling to each other in a foreign tongue as they cantered by.

I hurried round the cross, past the beggars asking for alms. I felt sorry, but I had nothing to give them, not even breadcrumbs. My stomach was growling so loudly I didn't hear the cart that nearly ran me over. The carter called me a pudding-brained jolthead. I was just thinking up a good insult to throw back when I caught my first glimpse of King Henry's palace and forgot all about the carter. I was standing outside the palace of the greatest king in the world – well, one of his palaces. He always seemed to be acquiring new ones. I must have looked like Jem the village idiot as I gawped at its walls and turrets and flags. His Majesty would be in there somewhere. If the Clerk of the Kitchen was in residence, then so was the King.

Then it finally dawned on me what my future had in store.

It didn't matter how splendid the place was, or how many kings were loitering in the halls, once I passed through the gates I'd be a kitchen boy and I wouldn't have anything to do with kings. And it didn't matter how much I tried to convince myself it would be all right. I was going to boil beetroot and chop turnips for the rest of my life. Even death in a ditch sounded more exciting!

I remembered how I used to picture myself leading the King's troops into battle and vanquishing his enemies. But that was just a boy's silly dream. Poor foundlings didn't get to lead the King's troops anywhere. Those close to His Majesty were of noble birth. But even as I thought this, I remembered the abbot railing about a certain Thomas Cromwell, one of King Henry's ministers. Father Busbrig hated him and was always going on about Cromwell's father only being a lowly blacksmith and a drunk into the bargain – which was rich coming from a man who swigged the altar wine whenever he could.

Anyway, Cromwell had started poor but he was fast becoming the King's most trusted man. If he could do it, then why not Jack Briars? I decided I'd find Master Cromwell and offer him my services. After all, the miserable old abbot thought I was going to get the door slammed in my face anyway. At least this way I'd be able to boast I'd had it slammed in my face by none other than the great Thomas Cromwell himself.

And there was just a chance that Master Cromwell would see beyond my straw hat, ragged shirt cuffs and jerkin that hadn't fitted me since I was eight. I felt a pang of regret for the pains Brother Matthew had taken with his letter which I wouldn't be using now, but I knew he'd forgive me – eventually.

A huge stone gatehouse towered over King Street. Set deep in its arch were two solid wooden gates, twice the height of a man on horseback, and carved like the portcullis of a castle.

I marched boldly up to them.

'Who goes there?' bellowed a voice from the shadows.

I nearly jumped out of my skin. I hadn't seen the man in King's livery until he slammed his staff onto the flagstones, just missing my toes.

'State your business,' he demanded.

'I'm Jack Briars, if it please you, sir,' I said. 'I'm here to work.'

'Well, I am His Majesty's Sergeant Porter, whether it pleases you or not,' said the man, staring at my ragged shirt cuffs, 'and I am here to chase away vagabonds, rascals and boys. And I'll warrant you are all three. On your way!'

2

Father Busbrig's smug face seemed to hover in the air in front of me.

The beslubbering old buzzard had been right. In fact, more right than he thought. The door hadn't even been opened to me, let alone slammed in my face. I wondered if the beggars up at Charing would lend me a bowl.

I was going to have to show my letter. It was the only thing that might get me past the Sergeant Porter. Brother Matthew would have breathed a sigh of relief to see me doing as I was told for once.

The man snatched the letter, produced a pair of eyeglasses and perched them on the end of his nose. His mouth turned down so far that he looked like one of the trout back in the abbey pond.

'*Dear Cousin,*' he read out slowly, '*I ask you to give employment to the bearer of this letter, Jack Briars. He is clean, godly and obedient . . .*'

He peered at me doubtfully over his glasses. I hid my surprise at my godfather's description of me. He must have done some penance for those fibs.

'. . . *a lively enquiring mind* . . .' the Porter continued.

Brother Matthew always said I was too nosy.

'. . . *and I ask you, Cousin William, to take him into your employ. You will not be disappointed.*'

The Sergeant Porter sniffed and slapped the letter into my palm. Without a word, he turned away and I heard the rattle of a key in a lock. He pushed open a small door in one of the gates and nodded for me to go through. *God's oath*, I thought, *I'm in!* and I charged forwards. But before I'd got a foot inside the royal courtyard a hand planted itself firmly on my chest.

'You will go straight to the kitchens and nowhere else,' barked the Porter, poking me in the ribs with each word. 'It's on your left, beyond the dairy and workshops. And mark this, it will not go well with you if you're found near the royal apartments. Understand?'

'Yes, sir,' I replied, because I *had* understood perfectly. I just wasn't going to do what he said. If I was to find Master Cromwell anywhere, it would be with the courtiers, not the servants.

The Sergeant Porter stood aside, grumbling under his breath about vagabonds. I stepped through the door and into the courtyard.

It was hard to miss the royal apartments that I wasn't supposed to go near. Opposite the kitchen and workshop buildings rose the huge palace itself. The white walls with their brightly painted doors and mullioned windows were covered in carvings of horses, dragons and huge roaring lions. It was the most impressive place I'd ever seen.

Clearly King Henry didn't think the palace was impressive enough, as all manner of building work was being carried out. But then, he had to entertain foreign monarchs and ambassadors and the like, not a lowly foundling who'd lived in a plain cold abbey all his life. Father Busbrig wouldn't have been pleased to see the wooden scaffolding, and men building new walls and slapping fresh plaster and paint over the old ones. It wasn't that he was a humble man. He would just have been jealous of all the gold leaf.

The courtyard was as busy as Acton Village on market day, with servants, horses and courtiers, dressed in the finest clothes. Well, the horses weren't, but even the servants had smart red uniforms with 'HR' on the tunics. A troop of yeomen guard marched past in a flash of crimson and silver breastplates. Over their shoulders they carried halberds with double-headed axe blades and sharp spikes. They were making across the courtyard to the palace.

I itched to follow in their wake but I could feel the Sergeant Porter watching me so I plodded off towards the kitchen. I looked back. He was still glaring in my direction. If I didn't get free of his eagle eyes soon, I'd have an apron on and a bucket of eels to chop.

Someone yelled, 'Make passage!' and I jumped out of the way of a fat man with an armful of firewood.

The man was on course for the royal apartments. Keeping the man's vast belly between me and the Sergeant Porter, I crept towards the palace.

The man walked up some tiled steps to an important-looking pair of arched doors with a miserable-looking stone angel above them and a miserable-looking yeoman guard standing on either side. Courtiers and servants were going in and out. My stomach suddenly lurched at the thought of what I was about to do, but I ignored it. I decided to stride in confidently, pretending I was with the firewood man. No one noticed my knees wobbling as I strode up the steps.

I found myself standing in a huge vaulted chamber. I glanced about nonchalantly, as if the massive tapestries, jewelled ceilings and shining golden statues were a common sight. Passages and doorways led off left and right and a wide staircase wound up in front of me. I wished someone had written a sign – 'This way to Master Cromwell'. I was just wondering who to ask when I heard a bellow from outside.

'Stop that boy!'

The two yeomen charged into the hallway. They didn't look miserable any more. They looked angry – angry enough to spit me on their halberds!

I ran.

I belted down the nearest passage, battling through a bunch of courtiers who were chatting and laughing and leaning against the walls. And all with nothing better to do than get in my way.

Brother Matthew often worried that I was too thin. He was wrong – my bony elbows were a useful weapon for forcing a path through a sea of doublets and gowns. Curses followed in my path.

I reached the end of the passage, skidded round the corner and charged up a staircase. I could hear the shouts of the guards behind and one thought kept pounding in my brain – *HIDE!*

But there was nowhere. I raced up and down flights of stairs. I didn't dare try any of the doors I passed. No one would give shelter to a vagabond. I cursed King Henry's builders, who'd spent too long carving fancy woodwork and slapping gold leaf everywhere, and not enough time making hiding places for boys on the run. The footsteps were coming closer.

'There he is!'

Behind me the two men seemed to fill the whole corridor. I sprinted up a spiral stairway and came to a tiny chamber with a single high window.

'You can't escape us now.'

I turned. The guard looming into view was a giant, at least two yards high. I took one look at the sharp blade of his halberd and leapt onto the windowsill. Flinging open the casement, I stepped out onto a narrow brick ledge and nearly fell off with shock.

I was teetering high over a garden full of ornate hedges. Beyond its wall flowed the grey water of the

River Thames. I'd need to grow wings to get out of this.

The tall yeoman had reached the sill. He grunted as he heaved himself up. At that moment I'd have given anything to be chopping eels in the palace kitchen.

Suddenly I heard an astonished cry. 'What are you doing, lad? You'll get yourself killed!'

Dizzily I peered down. I hadn't noticed the wooden scaffolding platform sticking out from the corner of the tower, a good fifteen feet below. It was covered with tools and piles of stone – and a crowd of workmen, who were staring up at me, their mouths open.

'Got you!' A hand shot out from the window.

I jumped.

3

Old Brother Jerome told me once that a drowning man sees his whole life pass before his eyes. Well, it's not the same for someone who's about to fall to his death. All I saw was the ground rushing up and all I felt was cold white terror!

I flung out my arms and somehow my fingers caught the edge of the platform. The structure shuddered as it took my weight.

Hands grasped my wrists and hauled me roughly onto the scaffolding. I stared up into a weather-beaten face.

'What game are you playing?' demanded my rescuer. 'Do you want to get us all killed? The scaffolding near collapsed!'

'Thanks for saving me,' I said quickly. 'I'm new here at Whitehall and . . . I took a wrong turn.'

The man gave a guffaw of laughter. 'Then I won't

ever ask you for directions, lad,' he said. 'If I want Southwark, you'll send me to the top of St Paul's steeple!'

A large window sprang open close to the platform and a red-stockinged leg appeared.

'Seize that villain!' came a shout.

Before the workmen had the chance to obey, I raced for a winch with a thick rope wound round its drum. It sat on the edge of the platform. If it was strong enough to haul up heavy baskets of bricks then I guessed it was strong enough to take one skinny abbey boy to the ground.

I grasped the rope and flung myself over the edge.

I'd imagined the winch would slow me down. I was wrong. The ground rushed up at such a speed I thought I'd bore straight through it. I landed with a thump and lay winded in a lavender bush. Above the shouts of the workmen, who were cheering me on as if I was in a race, I heard the angry voices of the guards.

I pulled myself out of the flattened bush and plunged into a dark alley between the palace and the river wall. Running footsteps behind spurred me on. At the end was a rough building that smelt of herbs and ale. This must be the stillroom. I skirted quickly round it, keeping to the shadow of the river wall.

I burst into a wood yard. Joiners were busy at work, sawing and stacking timber. I darted between piles of wood – ignoring the surprised cries – and out at the other end, only to find myself back in the courtyard where I'd started.

'Halt!' That was no rough joiner's voice. The guards had caught up with me. In desperation, I slipped inside the nearest door.

I took in the huge, smoky room with its roaring fire and smell of roasting meat that made my belly twist with hunger. It was the last place I wanted to be – the palace kitchen. A host of men and boys stood round a huge table, joking as they worked. At the far end of the kitchen an archway led into a passage, but I had no hope of reaching it without being seen. I dived between the men's legs and under the table.

Above the clamour, there was no mistaking the thud of the door banging open. Everyone fell silent.

'Where's the boy hiding?' came a shout. I recognised the voice of the giant yeoman.

A puzzled murmuring filled the air, like the buzzing of bees.

The yeoman only had to bend down and he'd see me. Then I realised that among the forest of legs around the table, there was a skirt. I was surprised that a woman should be working in the palace kitchen, but grateful that she did! I crept along until the skirt hid me from view.

'There be a multitude of boys here, Nicholas Mountford,' said a calm voice. 'Though they be in plain sight, every one. Here's James and Tom the log boys and . . .'

'I don't mean the boys who work here, Mister Sorrel. We're after a vagabond! He entered the royal apartments.' Nicholas Mountford strode about the kitchen, his thick soles creaking ominously on the flagstones. He came so close I could see the silver Tudor roses on his shoes.

As I crouched there, not daring to move a muscle, a hunk of bread suddenly dropped to the floor. *No one's going to miss this,* I thought. But I'd just taken a huge bite when a hand appeared, feeling around for the bread! And suddenly a wrinkled face was staring at me in horror. It was the woman who belonged to the skirt. She let out a shriek.

'What ails you, Mrs Pennycod?' asked someone.

'Is the scoundrel there?' That was the guard.

My heart was in my mouth.

Well, it would have been if my mouth hadn't been stuffed full of bread. I wanted to plead with her not to give me away but I just spat crumbs over the floor. So I tried to look as innocent as possible – not very easy when you're found hiding under a table with a guard on your tail.

To my amazement, the old woman gave me a wink.

'I saw a rat,' she called. 'That's all.'

She stood up. Mrs Pennycod had saved me!

'I'd be glad if you would leave now, Mister Mountford,' came the calm voice again. 'You burst in with some cock-and-bull story, stomping about and

17

holding up the work of the kitchen! The Court won't be happy to have their luncheon spoilt.'

The buckled shoes paused a moment, then turned angrily and headed for the archway.

'Shame on you, young Nicholas,' the old woman called as they left. 'You'll be going without a taste of my pies if you don't watch your step.'

Something suddenly dangled in front of my nose. It was a chicken leg – in Mrs Pennycod's hand. I took it and gave the hand a squeeze of thanks. I may not have looked innocent when she'd discovered me – but I must have looked hungry!

I ripped the meat from the bone with my teeth, slipped from under the table and scurried out, back the way I'd come. I heard exclamations of surprise as I shot by, but I heard no one calling the guard. Once outside, I flattened myself against the wall until I was sure I was safe.

As I saw it, I had three choices. I could go back into the kitchen, present my letter and live a quiet life. I could slip out of the palace and start my training as a beggar up at the Charing Cross. Or I could make one more attempt to find Thomas Cromwell.

I pulled my letter out and stuck it under the nose of a man hauling a high-backed chair out of one of the workshops.

'Urgent message for Master Cromwell,' I said importantly, hoping he wouldn't be able to read it. 'Can you tell me where I'll find him?'

'In his rooms,' panted the man. 'He always takes his noontide meal there. First floor in the palace yonder. River end.'

I stifled a laugh. I'd been there already – on the outside. I wondered if Master Cromwell had seen me whiz past on the winch.

'I'm taking this chair to a chamber along the passage from there,' the man went on. 'Help me carry it and I'll show you.'

I stowed the letter and seized one arm of the chair. This was a stroke of fortune. The man was going to take me right to my destination.

'Are you all right there, lad?' chuckled the man as I staggered under its weight.

'Yes,' I squeaked breathlessly. 'I'm stronger than I look.'

He steered me round the workshop and back along the alley.

'This is a short cut,' he told me. 'There's a door at the bottom of the tower and then it's straight up the stairs.'

It sounded simple but, as we reached the tower, a yeoman guard went by. He didn't look like one of my pursuers but I wasn't taking any chances. I ducked my head behind the chair arm.

'What's the matter?' demanded the man.

The yeoman had turned at his voice.

'Just a twitch,' I said, jerking about a bit.

The spiral staircase was barely wide enough for one

man, let alone a man, a boy and a chair. It took us some time to reach the first floor. My clothes might have been too thin for the cold of early spring, but I was sweating by the time we'd deposited our load. And I had to remember to keep twitching.

'Thanks, lad,' said the man. 'Now you want the last chamber down there.'

He nodded towards a carved wooden door at the end of the empty passage.

I took a deep breath. There was nothing to stop me reaching Master Cromwell. I straightened my jerkin and held my chin high, ignoring the worms that had suddenly made a nest in my belly.

I walked briskly towards the door and was just bracing myself to knock when a heavy hand suddenly clamped itself onto my shoulder and threw me to the floor. I found myself looking up at a mass of steel points. My pursuers had fetched reinforcements.

Nicholas Mountford towered over me, a nasty smile curling his lips.

'Got you at last!'

4

'You didn't need to chase me,' I croaked, my mouth suddenly dry. 'I have good reason to be here.'

Nicholas Mountford hauled me to my feet. I twisted out of his grasp, threw myself at the door and beat on it hard.

'Let me in!' I yelled.

The guards made a grab for me again.

I turned and thrashed out with my fists and feet. There was a grunt of pain as I caught the giant on the chin and a curse as I connected with another's ankle.

I heard the door open and spun round in hope. Big mistake! In an instant the yeomen had my arms pinned at my back.

A thin, mousy-haired boy was peeping round the door.

'My master wishes to know what this brutish noise

might be,' he said nervously. He looked astonished when he saw me writhing in the guards' grasp.

'Nothing to worry about,' panted Mountford. 'All is well. Just an urchin we're going to throw into the Thames.'

The boy nodded and the door was shut.

'Listen!' I cried. 'I'm on vital business.'

'Silence!' someone hissed in my ear. 'You're just a vagabond and a liar.'

I had no intention of being silent. 'I must speak to Master Thomas Cromwell,' I bellowed.

Hands grasped my wrists and ankles and I was dragged away down the passage, as helpless as a trussed pig.

'Wait!' a powerful voice came from behind. The yeomen stopped. I squirmed round to see who'd spoken. I glimpsed dark, fur-trimmed robes and plump hands covered in fine rings. Nearly breaking my neck, I twisted further and saw a grave face with piercing brown eyes. Somehow I knew this was the man I'd come to seek. This was Thomas Cromwell.

'Why all the commotion?' He had a commanding voice that made a thrill run through me. 'What are you and your friends about, Nicholas Mountford? My scribes are trying to work.'

I was determined to have my say first.

'Good day to you, Master Cromwell,' I called. 'Forgive me for not bowing, but as you can see I'm rather tied up. I have important business with you.'

'Hold your impudent tongue!' snapped the guard in charge of my legs.

'We beg pardon for the interruption, sir,' said Mountford. 'This rogue has given us the run-around. He's been running about the palace without permission.'

'And climbing on the scaffolding,' said another. 'We've had a deal of trouble following him.' He sounded angry. I'd have bet all the jewels in the palace he was annoyed to have wasted time chasing an urchin all over the place.

'If you'll excuse us, sir,' said Mountford, 'we'll throw him in the river and be done with him.'

I saw a flash of ruby as one of the plump hands signalled for silence. 'Unhand the boy.'

'But, sir—' protested the giant.

'Let him go, I say.'

They dropped me onto the hard, wooden floor.

'I will hear his story,' continued Cromwell calmly. 'If I do not like it, you can toss him into the Thames. Indeed, I'll help you do it.' He reminded me of a lizard, with his heavy-lidded eyes staring unblinking at me. 'Speak, boy. What is this important business?'

I scrambled to my feet, straightened my jerkin and touched my forehead politely.

'I have something for you, sir,' I said.

'You never told us that,' said Nicholas Mountford angrily.

'He's not to be trusted, sir,' spat another.

23

I ignored them, fixing my gaze on Master Cromwell. He gazed back steadily, his face showing no emotion. But somehow it gave me a glimmer of confidence.

'What I bring you is priceless,' I added.

'I'll be the judge of that,' he said gravely, holding out his hand. 'Give it to me.'

I took a deep breath. 'I bring you . . . myself, Master Cromwell.'

The man's hand fell to his side and his brow creased into a frown. I gulped. I had gone too far. The yeomen seized my arms again.

'I've come to work for you, sir,' I rushed on. My heart was beating like a drum. 'I, Jack Briars, offer you my talents, my skills . . .' I made him a sweeping bow – or as sweeping as I could in the guards' grip, '. . . and my undying loyalty.'

The silence that followed was so deafening it pounded in my ears.

I decided I might as well be hanged for a sheep as a lamb, so I added, 'And if you don't want me, I'll go to the King. I wager he'll take me on!'

5

Cromwell threw back his head and roared with laughter, rocking on his heels.

'Damn your cheek, Jack Briars!' he declared. He waved a hand at the guards. 'You can go. I'll deal with this . . . urchin.'

The men turned and marched away.

The door wasn't being slammed in my face. It was being opened. *Stick that in your pipe, Father Busbrig,* I thought.

I followed Cromwell into a large room. Two boys about my age sat at a table, earnestly scratching away with their quills. They kept their heads bent until their master had passed. Then they both looked up. One was the boy who'd opened the door earlier. I winked at him and he gave me a shy smile. The other, an older, weasel-faced boy, stared sullenly at me.

A man in warm robes sat at another table, near a roaring fire. He stood hurriedly.

'A small matter for me to deal with, Mister Scrope,' Cromwell told him.

The man nodded. 'Of course, sir.'

Master Cromwell led me through a narrow door into another, smaller chamber. Oak cabinets and chests lined every wall, and tapestries covered the panelling above. The leaded window panes were thick and sent odd patterns across the documents on the table. Although it was midday, two candles burned, turning the corners of the room into dark, secret places. The fire burned low. Cromwell sat down on a carved chair, placed his hands flat on the table and gazed at me, as if he could see straight into my mind. I suddenly felt it would be impossible to hide my thoughts from him.

'There is something in you that pleases me, Jack Briars,' he said at last. 'You have shown courage – and a deal of impudence.'

'Thank you, sir,' I replied. 'They are at your service – well, not the impudence.'

'I pray not,' said Cromwell solemnly. 'I'm impressed that you've fought your way to my door – and escaped the King's guard into the bargain. But what use can you possibly be to me?'

'I'm quick-witted,' I said without hesitation. As well as devouring all the puzzles and riddles that Brother Matthew used to give me, I'd learnt a whole list of clever ways to annoy the old abbot. And an even longer list of places to hide from his stick. 'I'm strong and agile,' I added. This was true. Some of my hiding places had required a lot of climbing.

There was a clatter of horses' hooves on the flagstones down in the courtyard below.

'I'm a good rider,' I lied. The one time the abbey mule had broken into a trot, I'd fallen off into a puddle.

'And I can read and write,' I said quickly, so that he didn't question me about my riding. 'I was brought up in St Godric's Abbey – near Acton Village – and my godfather, Brother Matthew Raynald, taught me well. It was he who sent me to work in the kitchens here. But I am better than that.'

'I have many well-tutored boys who wish to work for me,' said Cromwell. 'Boys of good family, which I see you are not. What makes you better than them?'

Brutal honesty was the only answer.

'Because I'm like you,' I said defiantly. 'Because I'm *not* of good family and therefore I have to fight for my future. Because I've nearly broken my neck jumping off the palace roof and risked being sliced through by a halberd just to reach you.'

Cromwell's lizard eyes stared, unblinking, at me. I felt cold fingers of dread clutch my stomach. He turned and walked around his table. Then he faced me again, hands resting on the polished wood.

'I will take the risk.'

I'd spent my life being the foundling with only my godfather to tell me I was worth anything. And now

27

here was this man, practically the most important person in the land, about to give me a job.

'I think you will make something of yourself, Jack Briars,' he said. 'You will be a scribe in my office.'

I felt a stupid grin spreading over my face. 'I cannot thank you enough, sir,' I said earnestly. 'I will prove to you that you've made a good choice.'

'You will start work right away,' said Master Cromwell. 'I'm sure Mister Scrope has some copying for you. This is a busy office. Your handwriting skills will be put to the test immediately.'

'Yes, sir!'

'You were brought up by monks. Are you an orphan?'

'I don't know, sir,' I said. 'I'm a foundling. Brother Matthew stumbled upon me when I was newborn. It was St John's Day and he named me John, though everyone calls me Jack.' There was nothing else for it. I had to tell him all even though it was an embarrassing story. 'I was hanging upside down in a bush by my swaddling clothes, yelling fit to burst with my bum hanging out. It was a briar bush – so I'm Jack Briars.'

I told him how Father Busbrig had taunted me about my start in life almost every day. 'He declared that my mother had been so disgusted at the sight of me that she'd thrown me away and had probably been aiming for the nearby compost heap!' I finished.

'Then it was lucky for you she missed,' said Cromwell dryly. 'It's useful that you can ride well,' he went on. 'I wouldn't have expected that from a boy brought up in an abbey. But then I wouldn't have expected him to clamber all over the palace like a squirrel, so perhaps I'm somewhat out of date with abbey education!'

Ah, the riding. I'd have to do something about that. It did seem an odd requirement for a scribe, but I wasn't going to question him. I certainly didn't want to be tested on whether I could stay in a saddle.

My new master turned to lead me out. I suddenly remembered Brother Matthew's letter for the Clerk of the Kitchen. I slipped it from my shirt, took a step towards the fire and dropped it into the flames.

I wouldn't be needing that now.

6

Cromwell ushered me into the scribes' office.

The weasel-faced boy was standing close by, earnestly reading a document. Something wasn't quite right with this scene. Had he been listening at the door? His whole demeanour seemed to shout it at me – that, and the fact he had the document upside down. He saw me looking and scuttled to a table.

'Jack Briars will be joining us as a scribe, Mister Scrope,' Cromwell told the man by the fire, who was busy chewing a chop. It made my stomach yearn for food. 'Set him to work immediately. Mister Scrope is the Chief Scribe here, Jack, and you'll do his bidding.'

He went back into his room without another word.

Mister Scrope rubbed his thin hands on his robe. They left trails of grease.

'Oswyn will show you where to sit and where you'll sleep tonight,' he called lazily.

I wondered which of the two boys was Oswyn. I soon found out. With an exaggerated sigh, the weasel-faced boy stood and swaggered over. He was taller and seemed to enjoy looking down on me.

'We sleep in here. It's first come first served, so I get the hearth. You'll be over there.' He pointed towards the furthest corner from the fire. 'No feather bed for you, but I doubt you'd know one if you fell over it.'

'There might be a space a bit closer to the warmth . . .' the other boy said nervously, tailing off as Oswyn curled his lip.

'Your two penn'orth is not wanted, Mark,' Oswyn sneered.

'Don't worry, Mark,' I said casually, ignoring Oswyn. I itched to put my fist in his face, but I had a feeling it wouldn't be wise on my first day. 'I've never slept in a room with a fire. Even the furthest corner will be luxury.'

'Of course,' hissed Oswyn. 'Foundlings are used to being out in the cold.'

So he *had* been listening at the door.

I stared back at him, not letting my gaze drop. Mark suddenly popped up between us and took me by the arm.

'Mister Scrope?' he called urgently. 'Shall I take Jack to get his livery and then to luncheon?'

The Chief Scribe dabbed at his lips. 'Indeed, Mark.' He sniffed loudly and cleared his throat. 'On the way back, pick me some mint. I feel a cold coming on.'

Mark led me out into the passage, down the stairs and through a maze of turnings.

'I'm Mark Helston,' he told me. His voice was hesitant, as if he was apologising for daring to speak. 'I couldn't believe it when I saw you fighting the guards. What was going on?'

'Just a misunderstanding,' I said vaguely. If I told him about the chase, it might be too much for his nerves!

'Well, you're very brave,' said Mark. 'But there's something I must warn you about. Be careful of Oswyn Drage. He doesn't like you.'

I laughed. 'I can see that!' I said. 'But I won't let it bother me.'

Mark stopped and stared earnestly into my face.

'You don't understand,' he said in a low voice. 'If Oswyn doesn't like you, he'll do everything he can to get rid of you.'

7

'By the devil!' I declared. 'Oswyn can try but he won't succeed.'

'Well said,' breathed Mark, but he didn't sound convinced. And I wasn't convinced either. Had I got rid of the bullying abbot from my life just to replace him with Oswyn Drage? Then I thought of something.

'How can he get rid of me?' I asked. 'Surely Cromwell's in charge, not Oswyn Drage.'

'Master Cromwell lets Mister Scrope sort out the scribes,' explained Mark, 'and as long as Scrope is filling his belly and the work's being done, he doesn't mind who's there to do it.' His eyes filled with fear. 'You won't tell him I said so?'

'Course not,' I assured him. 'How long have you worked in the scribes' office?'

'Since I was ten,' said Mark. 'That'll be three years in May.'

'And Oswyn?'

'He was already there,' said Mark.

'Have there been others in that time?' I asked.

'That's what I'm trying to tell you,' insisted Mark. 'Oswyn got rid of them. You're the sixth.'

'You're forgetting something,' I told him.

Mark looked puzzled.

'He hasn't got rid of you,' I went on.

'But that would be terrible.' Mark sounded very worried. 'My mother depends on my wage. My father's dead and there's no one else . . .'

'I don't think Oswyn would care about that,' I said. 'But somehow you've kept your job when others haven't. What's your secret?'

'I've never thought of it like that,' said Mark, brightening. 'I don't answer back when he bullies me and I just keep out of his way.'

'Then that's what I'll do,' I said.

I knew I wouldn't manage it, but Mark seemed relieved.

We crossed the courtyard I'd seen several times that day. Mark nervously made way for everyone. I longed to use my sharp elbows again but I gritted my teeth and followed him – at a snail's pace.

'We're going to the Master Tailor,' he said over his shoulder. 'Well, the workshop where his staff are. He's too important to bother with a scribe's uniform. Mister Wiltshire will help you. The Master Tailor deals with the King's clothes.'

'Do you see a lot of the King?' I asked.

'No,' said Mark. 'His Majesty has never been to our office.' He gave a nervous laugh. 'I think I'd die of fright if he did!'

'But you must have seen King Henry,' I persisted. 'What's he like?'

'Only from a distance,' said Mark. 'If Master Cromwell needs someone to carry papers to the royal presence, he always sends Oswyn, thank heavens. His Majesty is very big and very loud – and if he's in a rage he almost brings the ceiling down with his bellowing.' He shuddered. 'Even Master Cromwell is careful of His Majesty's tempers.'

We passed the wood yard.

'Why are those joiners staring at you?' asked Mark. 'Do you know them?'

'Er . . . in a way,' I answered quickly.

We entered a long passage close to the Great Kitchen.

'Here we are,' said Mark, opening a door halfway down. There were several men and boys inside, sewing and cutting cloth. We stood back to let a girl pass. She was carrying a pile of bed linen. It looked almost too heavy for her skinny arms. I wondered what it would be like to lie on fine sheets like those – well, to lie on a sheet of any sort!

One of the older men looked up. 'Hurry up, Cat!' he called, but he didn't sound cross. 'You've got to finish those cuffs for Sir Barnard Boniface after you've delivered those mended sheets. And no stopping to chat on the way.'

'As if I would, Mister Wiltshire,' the girl called back cheekily. She cast a brief glance at us.

'Hello, Mark,' she called and marched off down the passage.

I suddenly realised that Mark was standing frozen in the doorway, gawping like a frightened flatfish.

I shook his arm. 'What's the matter?' I asked. 'You look as if you've seen a ghost.'

'Much worse,' Mark croaked. 'That was Cat Thimblebee. She's the only girl in the sewing room, and I've heard she's a fiend if you cross her.'

I watched the girl go. She had bright red hair that bounced under her cap, and a very determined walk. Poor Mark. He seemed to be scared of everybody, from red-headed sewing girls to royalty.

I dragged him into the sewing room to collect my uniform.

JP

We walked back through the herb garden, past the lavender bush I'd squashed. Now I was dressed in my red livery I suddenly felt a thrill, knowing I could walk around the palace without the threat of a spike up my bum – and with dry feet, as I'd been given a pair of shoes with no holes in them. Mark picked a bunch of mint for Mister Scrope.

'It's our young death-defying friend!' shouted a voice.

A workman waved at me from the scaffolding. I gave him a grin as we went by.

'I wouldn't have recognised him in his fine clothes,' called another.

Mark gawped at me, open-mouthed. 'I thought you'd just arrived,' he said, 'but everyone seems to know you! What did he mean by *death-defying*?'

I couldn't go on avoiding Mark's questions for ever. I was going to have to give him an answer, even if he had an attack of the vapours.

'The guards were on my tail as soon as I got into the palace,' I explained. 'They cornered me in that tower, so I jumped out of the window.'

Mark's eyes were popping out of his head. And not just with fear. I concluded that he liked a tale of danger, as long as he wasn't the one in danger!

'But surely the drop should have killed you!'

I think he thought I was supernatural. For a second I wondered whether to leave it at that. 'I managed to grab hold of the platform below,' I admitted at last.

We were passing under the wooden scaffolding tower and I couldn't resist jumping up and grasping one of the horizontal struts. 'Like this!' I yelled as I swung my legs.

I heard Mark give a horrified gasp. A young man was coming round the corner. I knocked him flying.

8

I jumped down and ran to my victim, who was lying on his back in the mud. The fine velvet cloak and fur-lined robe gave me no doubt that I'd flattened one of King Henry's courtiers. He was purple with fury.

'Forgive me, sir,' I cried, offering a hand to help him up.

He slapped it away and got to his feet. I quickly recovered his hat from a puddle. The feathers were broken but I managed to brush most of the dirt off before I gave it back to him.

'You clumsy fool!' he snapped, aiming a clout at my head. I ducked instinctively and he missed. This made him angrier still.

'Don't you know who I am?' he demanded, white flecks appearing at his mouth as he spat out the words.

'No, sir,' I said. The man was short and stocky and

thrust his chin forward as he spoke. He reminded me of a chicken and I had a mad desire to laugh.

'I am Edmund Talbot.' The man paused, as if waiting for some recognition. I heard Mark give a faint whimper of fear. 'Everyone will know my name soon enough and you'll live to regret what you've done.'

He swept off, trying to look impressive, but his limp hat and the mud dripping from the hem of his cloak rather spoilt the effect.

'This is terrible,' wailed Mark. 'You knocked a gentleman down. And Edmund Talbot of all people! He dismisses his own servants for the slightest thing. Do you think he'll have us both thrown out?'

'It was just bluster,' I tried to reassure him. 'And if anything's said, I'll tell Master Cromwell you had nothing to do with it.'

'Thanks,' said Mark, looking relieved. 'But what about you?' He grinned shyly. 'I hope Talbot doesn't make trouble. I'd like you to stay.'

Mark reminded me of a faithful lapdog. If I let him, he'd probably trot round after me for ever! I wasn't going to turn away a possible friend. I didn't have enough of those in my life. In fact, I didn't have any, apart from Brother Matthew. I grinned back at him.

'I reckon Talbot won't say a thing,' I said. 'He won't want to admit he was knocked into the mud by a skinny little scribe.'

I didn't tell him how worried I really was.

'Are we to go straight to lunch?' I asked hopefully,

for although the rest of me was worried about Talbot, my stomach was still hoping to be fuelled.

'Follow me,' said Mark. 'We shall be eating in the Great Hall. That's where all the servants take their meals. Beware – it is very noisy and can harm the digestion.'

I was used to the silence of the monks' refectory so the clamouring chatter in the Great Hall was music to my ears. It certainly didn't harm my digestion. Mr Scrope nodded to us from behind a trencher piled high with food.

As soon as Mark saw him stand to return to work, he pulled me to my feet and we hurried off behind him.

Back at the scribes' chamber I took a knife and cut my quill to a point, ready for work. Mister Scrope looked over my shoulder as I copied out a simple bill for cheesecloth for the dairy.

'Very good,' he said, casting a brief glance at the first line. 'Oswyn Drage, you could learn something from Jack!' He went off to his table and his mint infusion, little knowing the effect of his words. Weasel-face looked at me as if he would shoot arrows from his glaring eyes.

But I had bigger concerns than a jealous scribe. I chewed the end of my quill, wondering how long it would be before Edmund Talbot got me sacked.

'Don't eat those feathers, Jack,' whispered Mark. 'I heard of a boy who did and they went straight to his belly and tickled him to death.'

'I'll be careful,' I whispered back.

I'd just finished my first page when Weasel-face got up from his seat and sauntered over to our table. As he leant over my work to take a fresh parchment, his sleeve caught my quill, sending ink splattering all over the completed account.

'Sorry!' he drawled. 'An accident.'

'That's all right . . .' I began to say. Then I caught sight of the gloating look on his face before he turned away and strolled back to his chair.

I knew it wasn't an accident. I itched to grab him by his scrawny throat, but saw Mark's anxious glance just in time. Mister Scrope tutted and threw me a rag so I scrubbed furiously at the ink instead, pretending it was Oswyn's ugly face.

'Well done,' muttered Mark as I finally began to make a fresh copy of the ruined document.

'Oswyn's nothing but an annoying fly,' I whispered. 'All buzz and no sting.'

Mark managed a smile. 'Just don't try to swat him,' he whispered back.

The door to the inner office swung open and Master Cromwell appeared. I had no time to hide the ink-splattered page.

'Come in here, Jack Briars,' he ordered sternly. 'I would speak with you.'

I heard Oswyn snigger.

I stood in front of Cromwell's desk, feverishly wondering what he was going to say. The spilled ink? Unlikely. Mark had said that Cromwell left the business of the scribes to Mister Scrope. Edmund Talbot must have spoken to my master.

I suddenly felt sick.

'You've been here merely hours,' said Cromwell.

'Yes, sir,' I agreed.

'And yet . . .' Cromwell paused as if considering something.

'Please give me longer to prove myself,' I blurted out. I was about to try and explain about the accident, but before I could he spoke again. His words astonished me.

'I intend to,' said Cromwell. 'I have an errand for you. Come to me early tomorrow morning.'

'Anything, sir!' I hoped my relief didn't show on my face. 'I will do my utmost to . . .'

'Do not waste time on fine words, Jack,' said Cromwell dismissively. 'Your deeds will prove whether they're true. I will be away from the palace on the morrow. Be here at dawn and I will tell you more.'

'Yes, sir,' I said, feeling pleased to be singled out for the task.

'And one more thing, Jack,' said my master.

'Sir?'

'Tell no one of this.'

9

I didn't sleep much in my allotted corner of the scribes' room. Oswyn snored loudly, his weaselly mouth open wide, and Mark muttered in his sleep most of the night. But that wasn't what kept me awake. My mind kept going over my luck – Edmund Talbot had been all mouth, and Cromwell had given me a mysterious task!

At dawn, as soon as I saw my master pass through our chamber to his own, I leapt up, pulled on my livery and reported to him.

Cromwell got straight to the point. 'You know the village of Kensington?'

I nodded. 'It's on the way to the abbey, sir. On the Reading Road. About an hour's walk.'

'As you reach it, there's a well at the back of a row of cottages.' My master took a leather pouch from his table and held it out. 'Place this behind the loose brick in the wall of the well. You'll know the brick by its chipped corner.'

'May I ask what's in this?' I said as I took it.

'You may ask nothing,' said Cromwell briskly. 'It is not for your eyes. Now go. Show no one what you're carrying.'

I tried to push the pouch up my sleeve. It fell straight out. I pushed it down the neck of my tunic. It tumbled out at the bottom.

'I do not want anyone to know that you are from the palace,' Cromwell told me, looking at my livery.

'I'll wear my old clothes,' I said. 'I've still got them, stowed under my blanket.'

Cromwell nodded. 'Come to me on my return, after sundown, to report that you've carried out your mission.'

As I got to the door he called me back. 'You told me you could ride,' he said. 'Go to John Burrows in the stables. He'll find you an old pony that befits a boy in rags.'

'Normally I would,' I said, without a second's hesitation, 'but I have a boil the size of a pine cone on my bum and it'll be torture to sit on a saddle.'

'Then of course you must walk,' said Cromwell smoothly. I had the strange feeling that my master suspected that I didn't know one end of a horse from the other. 'And when you have done your errand you may pay a visit to St Godric's. I will tell Mister Scrope you have gone to collect your possessions.'

'Thank you, sir!' I exclaimed in delight.

'Your godfather will be pleased to hear the news of your quick promotion from kitchen boy to scribe. And he is sure to give you a poultice.'

'A poultice, sir?'

'For the boil on your bum.'

♪

I was soon striding along the Reading Road.

If any of the workers in the fields had bothered to look up from their digging they'd have simply seen a boy in rags. They'd never have guessed I was the proud owner of a royal livery – now safely stashed under brambles in St James's Park. And they'd never have guessed I had a secret assignment from the King's most trusted advisor.

I fingered the pouch, wondering about the contents. It felt like paper. It must be a highly important message to be delivered so secretly. Was it a plea to stop a war? An order to start one? I certainly wasn't going to disobey orders and look.

I smelt chimney smoke and saw a church tower ahead. I was almost at Kensington Village. The first thing I came to was a smelly pigsty, standing at the end of a field, but beyond it I spotted the cottages Cromwell had told me about. My job was nearly done.

The pigs let out a sudden squeal. Something had disturbed them. I heard the crack of a twig and turned to see a glimmer of movement beyond the sty.

45

Someone was there – someone who didn't want to be seen. I suddenly thought of the pouch. I had to protect it. I ducked between the sty wall and a thick holly bush, biting back a curse as the sharp leaves pricked through my rags. I waited.

A cloaked and hooded man came into view. He strode round the pigsty, his boots squelching in the slurry that oozed from it. As he passed, he looked this way and that, as if searching. I kept perfectly still. At last the footsteps faded.

I strained for the slightest sound of the mysterious man returning, but all I heard was the sound of the pigs snuffling contentedly again. I tried to convince myself the man was waiting for someone else, but I had to be cautious.

If the hooded man had been watching me walking along the road, he'd have seen a thin, fast-striding boy in rags. The answer suddenly came to me. I could become someone else. I'd trick his eye. It had worked before. I'd once dressed up in a borrowed monk's habit and walked right past the unsuspecting abbot, my head bowed as if in prayer. It might work again. Unfortunately, the pigs didn't have any handy monks' robes but, not six feet away, by the end cottage, washing was spread over a bush.

A crook was propped against the sty. I grasped it, hooked a smock off the bush and slipped it on. It covered my rags. I didn't know if my pursuer had seen my face but I wasn't taking any chances. I smeared mud over my cheeks and hair, smock and breeches. At least, I wished it was mud.

I twisted my features into a grimace and hunched my shoulders to give myself a crookback. Then I hobbled out, using the stick as a crutch. My heart was thudding in my ears but I limped on, my head down as I skirted round the sty and made for the back of the cottages. Soon the well would be in sight.

I laughed to myself. Perhaps I'd imagined danger when there was none. Or perhaps the man was spying on me from some secret place, seeing only a poor, crooked swineherd.

Two hands suddenly seized me round the throat and a voice snarled in my ear.

'Give me the pouch!'

10

The hands tightened round my neck.

'Let me go,' I croaked.

The croaky voice fitted my pretence of being a crippled boy but in fact it was all I could manage. The man's fingers were like a blacksmith's vice around my windpipe.

'Give me the pouch,' he hissed again.

I was about to whack him over the head with my crook when he released his grip on my throat and seized my arms instead. My weapon fell to the ground.

'Don't hurt poor Simkins,' I pleaded. 'I must fetch food for the pigs or my master will tan my hide.'

He shook me so that my teeth rattled. 'Hand it over.'

'I don't know about no pouch.' The words were jerked out of me and I began to wonder if the pouch would be too!

I rolled my eyes in terror – and it wasn't all play-acting – but I took note of my attacker. If I got back to Whitehall alive, I would describe this villain to Master Cromwell. The hood hung down low over his eyes but he was a young man with dark hair and a neatly trimmed beard. This seemed odd, given his rough clothes.

'I know you have it,' he growled.

'You must want that other lad,' I wailed. 'He swept past me as if the hounds of hell were after him. He knocked me flying and I hurt my knee. I'm a good lad, sir, and I mean no harm to no one and never think to have harm done to me, but now I'm late and my master will beat me and my knee is hurting and I'm a good lad, sir, and—'

'Which way did the other boy go?' demanded my attacker.

I waved a shaky finger across the fields.

'Be off with you then,' said the man, pushing me roughly away.

I sensed his eyes were still on me as I limped off, hunched over my stick, towards the back of the cottages. At last I heard him stride away, muttering curses.

There was no doubt in my mind now. The pouch contained something very important.

Finally the well came into view. I hobbled towards its mossy stone wall and sat heavily on it, leaning forward as if exhausted. Under the cover of the smock I eased out the loose brick with the chipped corner, poked the precious pouch into the gap and rammed the brick back.

I'd done it. I crept back the way I'd come. There was no sign of my attacker. I shuffled off to the pigsty and flung the smock over the bush again. The smock's owner had helped with vital business for Master Cromwell, and probably for the King himself, but they'd never know that was the honourable reason it was covered in dung.

I set out for St Godric's. I had no doubt of my master's gratitude when he heard how I – or rather Simkins – had saved the vital letter.

When I reached the abbey, the sight of its crumbling stone walls made me halt in my tracks. I'd never noticed before how neglected my old home was. For the first time I was seeing it with the eyes of a visitor.

I looked over towards Father Busbrig's tower, the only part of the abbey that he ever spent money on. He made sure his living quarters were very comfortable. He'd be sleeping off his lunch in there, so I'd be safe from his bullying attention. I knew Brother Matthew would be tending his herbs in the garden behind the abbey. I crept through the arch and ran to the familiar stooping figure, who was cutting sprigs of rosemary.

'Jack!' My godfather let out a cry of delight. 'I've prayed for you every hour since you left.'

He enveloped me in a huge hug, then held me at arm's length, searching my face anxiously. 'I hoped you would have good news for me,' he said, 'but you seem agitated.'

Brother Matthew knew me too well. I had to keep my adventure from him, but it showed in my face. I didn't know what answer to give him.

Fortunately his attention was taken by the aroma of the sty. And then he noticed my grimy cheeks.

'You surely haven't got a job with the pigs!'

'Not exactly . . .' I started to say. My heart began to pound. Father Busbrig was bearing down on us, a look of disgust on his fat features. He'd already cut himself down a new stick, I noticed; a stick with lots of nasty knobbly bits. I wondered if he'd been keeping watch out of his window, waiting for me to come back in disgrace so he could use it on me.

I was still afraid of him and his beatings. And that made me angry with myself.

'I thought we'd seen the last of this brat.' The abbot's blubbery cheeks wobbled in fury as he swished his stick. 'What's he doing back here?'

11

'Jack is telling me about his new job, Father,' said Brother Matthew hurriedly.

'Your cousin's as stupid as you if he's given this good-for-nothing a job in the palace kitchen,' sneered the abbot. 'If Jack keeps it for more than a day, I'll fast for a fortnight.' He stuck his red sweaty face into mine. I recoiled at his rancid breath. 'As I told you when you left, boy, don't think you can seek bed and board here again.'

He suddenly became aware of the dung on my clothes and thrust me away. 'You don't smell of the kitchen. You stink of pig dung.'

I was going to enjoy watching the sneer die as he heard my news.

'You're right as always, Father Busbrig,' I said meekly. 'I haven't got a job in the palace kitchen . . .'

My poor godfather reeled with shock. I was about

to put him out of his misery but the abbot raised his stick.

'What did I tell you?' he snarled.

I was reeling in a big fat fish that flapped at the end of my line. It felt wonderful.

'. . . because I have a better one!' I finished triumphantly. 'I'm working for Master Thomas Cromwell.'

Father Busbrig's cheeks were now as purple as one of Matthew's best beetroots. He stood gaping at me, his mouth opening and closing without any sound.

'Lying little wretch!' he spluttered at last. 'No one who stinks that badly could work for one of the King's ministers.'

'I fell over in a farmyard on my way here,' I said. 'But I speak the truth about my job.' I was loving every minute of this.

The abbot's jowls twitched uncontrollably as he glowered at me with his baggy eyes.

'Your new master is Cromwell?' he spluttered. 'Thomas Cromwell? How is this possible? You've made up a tale to cover your shame!'

'I have not,' I answered, staring calmly back. 'Are you saying that Master Cromwell, the most important man at Court, has made a bad decision in employing me? I would show you his seal but he'll not thank you for doubting me when I tell him.'

I plunged my hand into my jerkin. It was a gamble. If he challenged me, all I could produce was a bit of dirty undershirt. I held his gaze. The abbot looked away first.

'There's no need for that,' he growled.

I thought of the beatings the wretch had given me over the years. Now I'd beaten him and I hoped it hurt him as much as his stick had hurt me.

I took great pleasure in turning my back on him. 'It's really true,' I told Brother Matthew. 'Thanks to your teaching I have a good enough hand to become a scribe for Master Cromwell.'

Tears sprang into my godfather's eyes. 'I'm so proud of you,' he managed to say.

'We're all proud of him, brother.' The abbot was smiling at me now! That had never happened before. It was hideous. He looked like one of the stone gargoyles over the chapel door. 'I'm sure you won't forget your friends here at St Godric's,' he simpered. 'I myself have always had your welfare at heart.'

'I shall certainly remember my *friends*,' I replied coldly. 'And Master Cromwell will wish to hear how well those friends are being treated.'

The abbot's stick twitched. I stood my ground. At last the old man let out a hissing breath and waddled off, his stick thumping angrily on the ground.

'He thinks he can use me to get favours from Court!' I muttered. 'Well, he has another think coming.'

Brother Matthew squeezed my shoulder. 'Come to my cell and tell me all about Master Cromwell and your job . . . and clean yourself up a bit.'

'Gladly,' I said. 'Though I don't have long. I must report to my master this evening.'

'Will you have time to show me Cromwell's seal?' asked Brother Matthew eagerly as we entered his tiny cold room.

'I don't have one,' I admitted, 'but it was the only way to convince Father Busbrig of the truth.'

'I'm sure you'll be forgiven,' said my godfather with a smile.

I felt a wave of love for this humble man. He'd cared for me and educated me like his own son. I hugged him.

'Oh, get yourself back to Whitehall,' he said, his voice choked with emotion.

જાજ

I bounced along on the back of a cart bearing timber. The carter had promised to take me as close to London as his route allowed. I was glad I hadn't really got a boil on my bum as it was very uncomfortable and I was sure that a splinter was sticking through the thin material of my old breeches.

At last, the carter clicked his tongue and the old nag trundled to a stop.

'This is as near as I go,' he called over his shoulder. He pointed to the grassland stretching out to our right. 'That's St James's Park. Straight across there and you can't miss the palace.'

'Thank you,' I said, jumping down.

'Are you sure you'll be welcome at the palace smelling like that?' he laughed. 'I've heard how King Henry loves his pork, but I don't think he'll relish the smell of the sty as well.'

I grinned at him and set off. It was nearly dusk as I crossed the broad open heath. I hoped Cromwell might think I'd done so well that he would tell me what had been in the pouch. The light was failing and I saw no sign of the palace so I swung myself up into the branches of a sturdy oak tree.

My tree towered over the rest. From the top I saw the dark shapes of the roofs and church towers of London and the glint of the River Thames as it flowed away to the east. And just where the river bent stood the palace, the royal flags flying from the gatehouses and tiltyard of Whitehall.

I wondered if I'd ever get to see His Majesty joust. I'd heard he usually won – and not just because he was King, but because he was an expert. As I pictured King Henry on an armoured stallion, galloping full pelt and carrying a massive lance to unseat his opponent, I could almost hear the pounding of hooves.

Then I realised I *could* hear the pounding of hooves! I looked over the darkening heath, suddenly wondering if my pursuer had found a handy horse and caught up with me, for a horse and rider were certainly charging towards my tree. But they were coming from the direction of the palace, and I was relieved to see that the rider was only a servant girl, cloak flying wildly behind her. She sat astride the horse, like a farmer's wife, yet I suddenly realised that she was on a gentleman's horse, a handsome beast with a fine leather bridle. As quickly as they'd appeared, the horse and rider passed beneath the tree and up the hill beyond. But I'd have known that red hair anywhere. It was Cat Thimblebee, the girl from the sewing room.

What was she was doing riding such a magnificent horse? She must be stealing it! So now I had a theft to report to Master Cromwell as well as the success of my mission. He'd soon find that Jack Briars was indispensable, no matter what complaints Edmund Talbot might have.

As I climbed down the tree I heard a distant whinny. The horse was rearing up against the fading light in the western sky. A second later it had turned and was charging towards my tree again, the girl urging it on with excited whooping sounds. Hardly the behaviour of a horse thief, I decided. I watched the horse gallop back in the direction of the palace. So there was no theft to report after all, just a seamstress exercising a courtier's horse – unusual, certainly, but probably not criminal.

I retrieved my livery from the brambles, quickly changed and returned to Whitehall, carrying my old clothes. I was surprised to see that everyone I passed in the palace corridors stepped smartly back as I went by. *Of course,* I thought to myself, *they've all heard about the daring boy on the scaffolding.* Then

57

I realised they were staggering back at the pong of my rags!

'Faugh!' exclaimed Oswyn, flapping the air in front of him when I appeared at the door. 'You reek of the farmyard!'

Mark looked as if he was going to be sick!

I ignored them both and knocked on Cromwell's door. When he called for me to enter I stepped in, wondering too late if I should have left the clothes somewhere. Oswyn's table would have been the best place.

But my master did no more than raise an eyebrow at the whiff that followed me in.

'I've come to report to you as ordered, sir,' I said. 'I swear no one can have known my mission – and yet I was followed. A man attacked me and demanded I hand over the pouch.'

'And did you?' asked Cromwell, a deep frown appearing on his forehead.

'No indeed!' I exclaimed. 'I pretended I didn't know what he was talking about.'

I began to tell him what had happened. He listened calmly. I was just re-enacting Simkins – with a little exaggeration – when the door flew open and a hooded man burst in.

It was my attacker!

12

There was no doubt in my mind. The villain had followed me and now Cromwell was in danger. I had no weapon to protect my master. But the man hesitated when he saw me and those few seconds gave me time to think. I threw my stinking rags in his face and, as he staggered about blindly I launched myself at him. I saw with satisfaction his surprise as I brought him to the floor, along with three books and a candlestick from a nearby table. I sat on his chest and tried to force his arms hard against the floor.

'Fetch the guards!' I yelled. 'This is the man who was after me!'

I expected Master Cromwell to rush to the door, but he just stared at us. He might be clever, but he wasn't very quick in a crisis!

The man beneath me gave a strange smile, and the next moment I found myself flipped over and held fast.

I kicked and squirmed but he was too strong. I was just wondering if it was worth pretending I'd suddenly died of apoplexy so he'd loosen his hold, when I saw the fallen candlestick. I managed to grasp it between my fingers and was about to bring it down on his head . . .

'Enough!'

At Cromwell's words the man let go his hold and jumped to his feet, casually brushing away the rushes from the floor that had stuck to his clothes.

'I imagine you feel a little puzzled, Jack,' said my master calmly.

For a moment I just stared at them both. My attacker was watching me, the beginnings of a smile on his face. Rage started to boil up inside me. I felt as if I'd been used as a puppet in some sort of game I didn't understand. But a small spark of sense told me that losing my temper would not serve me well.

'I *am* puzzled, sir,' I said as calmly as I could. 'But I trust you have good reason to use me in this fashion.'

Cromwell seemed satisfied with my reply. He nodded and placed a hand on the other man's shoulder. 'This is Robert Aycliffe. He's training to be a lawyer, but he does other work for me too. The errand I sent you on was a test . . .'

'A test?' I repeated.

'. . . which you passed with full marks,' added Robert Aycliffe. He wiped away a smear of pig dung from his face. I was pleased to see that it spread further across his cheek.

60

'When you came to my door, Jack, I sensed you had the wit to be more than a scribe,' explained Cromwell. 'You had a certain manner about you – and then the yeoman Nicholas Mountford told me more about your . . .' he raised an eyebrow '. . . *exploits* on the day you arrived. But I wanted to be absolutely sure.'

'And the pouch . . .' I began.

'. . . held nothing but a piece of blank parchment,' said Cromwell, 'as you would have discovered, had you disobeyed me and looked inside.'

'Master Cromwell set me to waylay you,' said Aycliffe, 'and when I caught you, you had the wit to fool me.' He rubbed his shin. 'You're good at fighting too.'

'Thank you,' I said. 'I was merely protecting my master, as a loyal servant should.' I grinned. 'I'm sorry about your face, sir.'

Aycliffe looked confused.

'The pigs have left their mark,' I told him, pointing to the smears. I was enjoying knowing that this courtier stank as badly as I did. It paid him back for the trick he'd played on me.

Aycliffe wiped his hand over his cheek and smelt it. 'God's oath! I must ask your leave to go and clean myself up, Master Cromwell. I'm sure our paths will cross again, Jack Briars.' He made Cromwell a bow and was gone.

'Let me explain further,' said my master. 'As you know, my duties for the King are various but the most important is keeping our beloved monarch and country safe. Enemies lurk everywhere. You've proved you have the skills to help me. Are you willing to undertake an extra, most secret task now and again?'

I could scarcely believe what he was offering me. 'Yes, sir,' I declared. 'I will undertake any task you give me. I know I have the makings of a good spy.'

'Spy?' said Cromwell, his tone hardening in an instant. 'I spoke not one word about spies!'

'I'm sorry, sir,' I stuttered. 'I thought . . .'

'You are getting ahead of yourself, boy. I just ask that you follow my orders without question. Can you do that?'

I nodded, trying to keep the excitement growing inside from showing on my face.

'And remember this,' my master went on. 'The special work you will do must never be known to anyone. Even our monarch himself is not privy to all. In the eyes of the Court you are a scribe. Nothing more.'

'I won't tell a soul, sir,' I assured him.

'You are over-eager to agree to my terms, Jack,' said Cromwell. 'Wait until you've heard the whole. Your jobs will be small, and may seem petty, but each will have an important purpose. We are being watched all the time by enemies of this country. Enemies who would stop at nothing to know our secrets. Are you absolutely sure you are willing to risk your life in the service of your King? Think on that before you answer, Jack Briars.'

His words echoed in my head and my stomach tightened. There was something in Cromwell's voice that I couldn't ignore. This wasn't an idle threat made to scare a child. My master knew well what he was talking about. Although he didn't use the words, his tone spoke of treachery and death.

If I said yes, it would be like leaping from the scaffolding again, not knowing if I was going to be saved or smash my brains out on the flagstones. But if I didn't, I had the terrible feeling I would regret it all my life.

'I can think of nothing nobler than to offer my life to the King,' I said gravely.

Cromwell's eyes twinkled. 'Did you hear that in a mystery play?' he asked. I frowned. 'I'm making fun of you, boy, but I am pleased with your answer. Indeed, you had no choice but to accept. You have learnt too much about our special work.'

I didn't like to ask what he would have done if I'd said no.

There was a scratching at the door.

'Come in,' called my master. Weasel-face strode into the room, carrying a pile of documents. He looked round avidly at the mess on the floor. He must have heard the fight.

Cromwell thrust a letter towards me as if he was in the middle of giving me an order. '. . . and you will make five copies, Jack. But first you'll pick up all these things you have so carelessly knocked over. What is it, Oswyn?'

'The accounts from the Tower, sir,' said Weasel-face.

Cromwell waved a hand at the table. Oswyn put the pile down. He looked smug as he left – if a weasel can look smug. He'd soon be telling everyone how useless the new boy was proving to be.

'You may go, Jack,' said Cromwell. 'There will be another task for you tomorrow evening. A proper task, this time – with no tricks.'

'I'll be ready!'

'One more thing, Jack.'

'Yes, sir?'

'Wash those rags before their stench drives us all from the palace!'

13

I was early at my desk the next morning, waiting for my important mission. But as the morning dragged on, Master Cromwell stayed in his private office and I heard nothing from him.

Lunchtime came and went. I found myself turning every time Mister Scrope got up or the outer door opened. By the afternoon I could barely keep still in my seat.

'What's the matter?' asked Mark in a murmur. 'Have you got fleas?'

'I hope not,' I said. I forced myself to stop fidgeting.

'So do I,' said Mark earnestly. 'Mister Scrope will have you dipped in vinegar.'

'Does that get rid of them?' I asked, glad to have something else to think about.

'I don't know,' said Mark, 'but it burns like the fires of Hell.'

I grinned at him. He wasn't a bad sort, if a bit timid. I was willing to bet that Master Cromwell never sent Mark on secret missions if the thought of vinegar was enough to scare the breeches off him.

I was just writing an order of gold leaf for the King's new bathroom when Mister Scrope appeared at my elbow.

'Master Cromwell is leaving for Lutterall House within the hour,' he began.

I wasn't quite sure why he was telling me, but I thought I'd better sound interested.

'Lutterall House?' I said. 'Is that where he lives?'

'Ignorant country boy,' sighed Mister Scrope. 'Everyone knows that Master Cromwell lives at Austin Friars in the city. No, the King is to visit Sir Ralph Lutterall in two days' time and planning to stay at least a week. Our master must go to Hertfordshire ahead of His Majesty to make sure everything is properly prepared.'

A leaden lump of disappointment lay heavy in my belly. If Cromwell was off somewhere, he must have forgotten all about my next task.

'Before he goes,' Mr Scrope went on, 'Master Cromwell wishes to see you, Jack.'

Curse the man! He could have told me that first. I got to my feet.

Oswyn looked up hopefully. He thought I was in trouble again.

'No doubt our master wants my advice before he

goes,' I muttered as I sauntered past to Cromwell's door.

Cromwell was putting documents into a saddlebag. 'Your task,' he said shortly, as I entered. 'There's a man at Court who is giving me concern.'

'What's he done, sir?' I asked.

'He is said to have spoken ill of the King,' said Cromwell, taking a fur robe from his chair and putting it on. 'He may be a foolish blabbermouth who means nothing by his words. However, my job is to prevent trouble, so I must know exactly what he has been saying. Even if it seems trivial to you, I will require all the details.' He cast his eyes about the office as if making sure he had all he needed. 'The King dines tonight with the Court and of course I will be at Lutterall House. Your job is to act as my ears and eyes at that feast, where this man's tongue will be loosened by drink. He is careless, and careless men take no notice of servants when spilling their secrets.'

'And what will happen if he *is* speaking ill of the King?'

'Traitors are dealt with,' said Cromwell tersely.

Just four words and yet they felt as heavy as anvils. It struck me that whatever I reported back to my master might have serious consequences for this man. Traitors lived for long, painful weeks before they were put to death.

Cromwell was still speaking. 'Report to me on my return next week. You need to know nothing more.

You need to *do* nothing more. Do you understand?'

'Yes, sir. Who is this man?'

'His name is Edmund Talbot,' said Cromwell. 'Do you know him?'

I still had a vivid image in my head of the angry courtier with the mud dripping off his cloak. Talbot was sure to remember me, but I wasn't going to tell Cromwell that or he might give the job to someone else. No doubt he had many men working secretly for him.

'I've seen him about,' I said truthfully. 'He's a young man, short, of stocky build and' – I couldn't resist it – 'he thrusts his chin out like so when he moves.' I did an impression of Edmund Talbot's chicken walk.

'That's him,' laughed Cromwell. Then he gave me that look. The one that made me feel he was reading my mind and knew I was not telling all. 'You have sharp eyes, lad.' He picked up his saddlebag and made for the door.

'The King is holding his feast in the Presence Chamber. I have offered you, Mark and Oswyn to Mr Sorrel, the head cook, to serve at table. It is something we often do and will give you the perfect cover to be there. Mark will tell you about your serving duties. I will hear any news on my return.'

And he was gone.

I stood staring at his empty chair. I sensed that, though real, this task was another test. One which I had to get right.

68

14

I was on my feet the moment Mister Scrope dismissed
us at the end of the day.

'Why are you so eager for more work?' Oswyn
growled at me. 'My evening is ruined. I was going to
play cards with some gentlemen, something an abbey
boy like you will never do.'

'I'd rather earn a little extra than risk it at the card
table,' Mark whispered, as he followed me to the
door.

'Boys,' Mister Scrope called after us, 'save me some
raisin tarts. Not the plain ones – the honeyed sort.'

We left Weasel-face dragging his heels and muttering
about how his family was too good to serve at table,
and hurried to report to the head cook.

'What do we do at the feast?' I asked Mark as we
went. 'I wouldn't want to upset King Henry by getting
things wrong.'

'We won't be anywhere near His Majesty, thank God,' said Mark fervently. 'We'll be put down the other end, where the lesser courtiers are placed. The King will be served by his own servants and his food comes from the Privy Kitchen. We just have to keep the gentlefolk well supplied with food – and, remember, no one gets served before the King.'

I didn't think it would be too hard.

'And afterwards,' Mark went on, 'we eat anything that's left. And as the kitchens always make too much, it's a good supper!'

I liked the sound of that.

'Are you asked to do it often?' I inquired hopefully.

'I'm always glad of the extra pence that feast work brings,' said Mark. 'Even though it's not very often and I'm not very good at it. I always worry I won't be fast enough for the gentlefolk or that I might drip gravy down their necks.'

'Has that ever happened?' I asked.

'No, praise be,' he said. 'But there's always a first time. Just imagine if—' He broke off suddenly.

Cat Thimblebee had come round the corner, carrying a basket of bread and cheese. Mark gulped and pressed himself against the wall.

'No need to look so scared, Mark,' she laughed. 'I won't bite!'

I stayed where I was – right in her path.

'Good evening,' I said.

She looked disdainfully at me and tried to pass.

'I saw you in the park yesterday evening,' I went on. 'It must be wonderful to ride like that.'

Cat's green eyes flashed around as if to make sure no one had heard my words.

'You must be mazed to say such things!' she snapped. 'I know all about you, Jack Briars. You're a jumped-up nobody from an abbey who goes around trying to cause trouble.'

'Who's been telling you such tales?' I demanded.

'Oswyn Drage,' she said, shoving me aside. 'I overheard him talking to someone in the dairy just now.'

So my fame is spreading, I thought bitterly. I looked round for Oswyn to have it out with him, but there was no sign of the weasel. He was probably skulking back in the shadows. I pretended to laugh the girl's words off. 'Don't believe anything that dolt says. I did mean it, you know. You were really good on that horse.'

'Listen hard!' said Cat, through gritted teeth. 'It wasn't me.' She marched off without a backwards glance.

I watched her go. I was sure it had been Cat Thimblebee I'd seen riding the black horse but here she was denying it. Perhaps she just didn't want to have anything to do with me, after having heard what Oswyn had to say.

Mark seemed relieved she'd gone. He began to chat again as we walked along the passage, but I couldn't get Cat's expression out of my head. Not her angry, disdainful look, but her panic when I'd asked her about the riding. I realised I'd been slow-witted. She was a rude, opinionated girl, but underneath her anger she'd been really frightened. I'd wager anything that she wasn't supposed to be riding courtiers' horses. She must think she'd be in horrible trouble if I told. I decided to let her stew for a while.

I followed Mark into the Great Kitchen, recoiling as the heat hit me.

'Well, bless my soul, look who it is!' came a familiar voice. A small, squat figure was elbowing her way through the bustling servants. It was Mrs Pennycod, the pie maker. I hadn't realised how tiny she was!

She nodded to Mark and stretched up to whisper in my ear, her eyes full of laughter. 'Last time we met was under the table! Now I can see what a fine-looking boy you are, dressed in your livery.'

'Thank you for not giving me away, Mrs Pennycod,' I whispered back.

'Don't say I said so, but those guards get above themselves,' she said. 'And, anyway, you reminded me of my niece's boy, with your blue eyes and dark hair and always hungry, no doubt.' Her face fell for a moment, so that the lines deepened on her wrinkled cheeks. 'I don't see my family much. They live too far away. What's your name, lad?'

So news of the dreadful abbey boy hadn't reached Mrs Pennycod's ears at least!

'Jack Briars,' I told her.

'Jack suits you,' she said. 'You're a right Jackanapes – plenty of cheek!' She turned to Mark and squeezed his arm. 'You've picked yourself a good friend here, Jack.'

I could see that Mark was pleased with this but he also looked a bit confused.

'How do you know Jack, Mrs Pennycod?' he asked.

'We met yesterday,' chuckled the old lady. 'But we didn't have time to be properly introduced! Now, I expect you're hungry.'

She took two apples from a nearby basket and handed them to us.

I munched gratefully. Mark might have promised that we'd eat well at the end of the feast, but that was hours away and I'd been anxious on behalf of my stomach, which always seemed to be rumbling.

'Is there anyone at Court you haven't met?' whispered Mark.

Oswyn swaggered in, took an apron, thrust one at Mark and slung one my way. I caught it deftly.

Mrs Pennycod frowned. 'That's enough of that!' she told him. 'We don't throw things in this kitchen.' She took the apron and tied it firmly round my middle.

'So, Jackanapes,' she said, 'you'll be one of Master Cromwell's boys, come to serve in the Presence Chamber tonight. You've done well for yourself.'

She reached up a gnarled hand and patted my cheek.

A man was walking about the kitchen, inspecting the platters of pigs' heads and venison and carp and other fancy food, some of which I'd never seen in my life. 'Is that William Thynne?' I asked Mrs Pennycod. 'He's cousin to my godfather.'

'Bless you, boy,' she chuckled. 'Mister Thynne is the Clerk of the Kitchen. He's too important to bother with the everyday cooking. He sees to the accounts and buying of spices and whatnot. No, that's Mister Sorrel, the head of the kitchen. You must report to him now.'

So these were the important feet that had sent Nicholas Mountford on his way when I was hiding under the table.

I was soon following Mister Sorrel and the other servants along the passages. It was a way I'd never been before, but it kept us out of the cold night air. I sniffed up the wonderful smell from my heavy plate of pigeon pies. One pastry edge had fallen off. I was just wondering if I could lean forward and take a nibble without anyone noticing when we got to the Presence Chamber. I looked up from my pies to see a huge, high-vaulted hall, with stained-glass windows lit by hundreds of candles and crackling fires in the hearths. The stained glass showed the saints, and not one of them appeared pleased to be there – but then it's no easy task being a saint. Opposite the saintly windows, Greek heroes were fighting each other all over the walls, trampling on rather a lot of dead bodies as they did so.

Suddenly there was a blast of trumpets and the

courtiers jumped to their feet, bowing and bobbing. King Henry had arrived for the feast.

As the King entered, I found myself transfixed. The man was magnificent. He wore a gold tunic and he seemed to be covered in rubies. I'd thought Nicholas Mountford was a giant, but the King eclipsed everybody. I understood why he would win at jousting and anything else he turned his hand to. He was red-headed and broad-shouldered and looked as strong as an ox. But it wasn't only his strength that had me gawping. King Henry oozed power.

He took his seat at a long table laid with a white embroidered cloth. A dark-haired lady sat next to him. I'd heard about Lady Anne Boleyn. She was the woman he would marry if he could get a divorce from his wife, Katherine. The King needed a son and Queen Katherine had only produced one daughter, Mary. I had heard Father Busbrig declare Anne Boleyn an ugly witch who had supplanted the true queen, but she didn't look like a witch at all. However, I was surprised that her clothes were plain, just a simple blue dress with wide sleeves. Her only jewellery was a fine choker with a golden letter B. Then I realised that the simplicity was a clever move. She was being careful not to outshine her monarch.

Endless servants, special ones just for the King, were bringing platters of food that had certainly not come from the Great Kitchen. A small, skinny man leapt in front of the King's table and made him a mocking bow.

He was dressed all in green and he carried a cow's horn in one hand.

Mark appeared at my shoulder. 'That's Will Somers,' he said when he saw my surprise at the man's rudeness. 'Or have you already made friends with him too?'

I shook my head. 'Who is he?' I asked.

'He's one of the King's fools,' whispered Mark. 'He can take liberties with His Majesty that no one else would dare to.'

There was a roar of laughter from the royal table, the King louder than the rest. Will Somers doffed his cap then moved on to another table.

'I don't know why Mr Somers is called a fool,' said Mark. 'He's a very clever man, full of wit. I sometimes think he's even closer to the King than Cromwell. His Majesty certainly listens to his counsel, or so I've heard.'

If that was true, I wondered if my master envied the King's fool. But I couldn't see Cromwell blowing a horn and capering about in a green suit.

I remembered my mission and quickly ran my eyes over the noisy courtiers at the long tables around the sides of the chamber. I was just wondering how I'd ever find Edmund Talbot when I noticed Mister Sorrel signalling impatiently to me. He jerked a thumb towards a table at the far end of the room. Without thinking, I took the quickest route, walking in front of the royal party. Oswyn appeared at my heels, breathing down my neck. I was about to tell him to give me a bit of space when he suddenly hooked a foot round mine. As trips go, he did well. I went flying forwards, my mind registering one horrific thought.

Me and my pies were hurtling straight at the King!

15

I did the only thing I could think of. I slammed the platter onto the table. Unfortunately, I was right in front of King Henry. But at least I'd stopped falling and so had the pies. Except for one, which catapulted off the plate and spun in the air, making straight for the royal head.

I made a desperate lunge and caught it just in time. I'd saved my monarch from a face full of pigeon. I landed on the table, next to my pies.

A surprised gasp rippled round the King's table. I prostrated myself on the floor.

'By St George!' came a deep voice. I looked up to find the King peering over the tablecloth at me. His eyes were sparkling with amusement. 'Well caught, young man. Tell me, what is your name?'

'Jack Briars, Your Majesty,' I told him as I scrambled to my feet. I was surprised he heard my answer over the knocking of my knees.

'Where is Will Somers?' called Henry. 'Come hither, Will. You could learn much from Jack Briars' capers.'

Will Somers left the courtiers he was entertaining and solemnly looked me up and down. Then he looked at the mess on the royal table.

'Verily a clever youth,' he said. 'Tell me, young sir, what is in the pies?'

'Pigeon, Mister Somers,' I answered.

'Then I bow to thee for giving those birds new wings!' He blew on his horn and swept me a bow. Everyone erupted into laughter and the King dismissed me with a wave of his hand.

I grabbed the platter and made for the end of the chamber where I'd been instructed to stand. I passed Robert Aycliffe, now looking every inch the courtier in a velvet doublet, and with no sign of any pig dung. Oswyn was already in his position, waiting for the order to serve the courtiers. He glowered at me as I went past. Mark was serving a woman who was dressed all in lace. He looked terrified – even though he had only bread on his platter and no gravy to spill down the fancy gown. But where was my target?

I took my place behind a long table. One voice was raised above the others. I knew those ranting tones, and soon spotted Edmund Talbot. He was seated only a short distance from where I stood, but as far from the King as was possible. Clearly he was not considered very important at Court.

I moved a little closer. Like his companions, Talbot was dressed in fine clothes, with a heavy gold chain arranged across his shoulders. His cheeks were flushed and he lurched about on his bench. He was drunk before the glasses had even been filled.

I was about to sidle up to Talbot when I was summoned by a portly old man who practically took up two places on his bench.

'Boy! Bring me the largest pie on your platter.'

He already had a plate piled high with spinach tart and slices of beef. I served him quickly then moved back towards my target. Talbot was railing at anyone who would listen, waving his goblet about as he spoke and splashing his neighbours with wine.

'Be warned,' he was saying, 'there'll soon come a day when none of you will want to cross me!'

I listened intently.

'Hush, Edmund,' said the man next to him, wiping drops of wine from his white shirt cuffs. 'You're speaking very loudly. Take care not to disturb the King.'

'If I were you,' Talbot went on, his speech slurring, 'I'd take care too. Take care to make the right connections while you can. In fact, I'll warrant you'll soon be begging to be my friends.' He waved a hand round the table. 'All of you!'

He punctuated this by slamming his goblet on the table.

'You're ever quick to tell us so, Edmund,' said the

man on his other side. 'And ever quick to tell us you're going to be raised to high office one day. But we won't hold our breath waiting.'

'You're more likely to rub shoulders with His Majesty's jailers if you don't curb your tongue,' added another.

'You'll be sorry for that!' spat Talbot, throwing out a hand and knocking the man's drink flying.

The man rose as if to strike him but his neighbour took him by the arm. A servant mopped up the spilt wine.

It seemed to me that Talbot was just a drunken bag of wind, making wild threats no one believed. But Cromwell had told me to report whatever I heard so I made a mental note of all he said.

I waited to hear more but the portly old man called me back. He was outraged that the platters in front of him were empty when he'd hardly had a mouthful, or so he said. I reckoned there was a full meal nestling in his beard but I thought I'd better not say so. Feeling irritated with his demands, I offered him another pie.

'I've had a surfeit of those,' he complained. 'Fetch me some manchet bread, boy, before I starve to death!'

I looked about to see if I could find someone else to fetch the bread. I didn't want to miss any of Edmund Talbot's words.

Talbot was flapping his arms about like a windmill now, almost flooring the servant who had appeared at his side. He began to shout at the man, but suddenly saw that he was holding out a letter. He snatched it and smiled broadly as he read. Then he rose, threw down his napkin from his shoulder and left the table.

I started after him but had to make way for a group of tumblers who came cartwheeling into the room, to great applause. When they'd gone by, I realised that Edmund Talbot was slipping out of the door which they'd come in. I was amazed. Even though I'd only been at Court a few days, I knew that courtiers never left the King's presence without his permission. There must have been something in that letter to make him behave so rashly. I tried to catch sight of the servant who'd brought it but he was gone. My master hadn't told me that I must trot after Talbot wherever he went. In fact, he hadn't told me to follow the man at all – just to listen to his talk at the feast. But, I reasoned, I couldn't do that if I was inside the Presence Chamber and he wasn't. I was certain that Cromwell would want to know exactly why Talbot had left the feast so stealthily – and, to tell the truth, so did I!

'My bread!' The portly old man was waving a chubby hand.

'I'll fetch it immediately,' I said. It was the just the excuse I needed to leave the Presence Chamber.

I passed Mark as I left. 'Fetching more bread,' I told him.

He nodded. I knew he'd have been worried if he'd seen me leaving without permission, and now I had someone else to back up my story.

My way out of the Presence Chamber was blocked by a man carrying a huge flagon of wine. By the time I'd got past him, the passage outside was empty. I'd lost Edmund Talbot.

16

I sprinted along to the end of the silent passageway and listened for footsteps. Someone was climbing the stairs ahead. I remembered that this part of the palace looked out over the compost heap, and was where the less favoured courtiers slept, so Talbot might well be going to his chamber, though I couldn't think why a letter would summon him there.

I'd just reached the top of the stairs when I heard someone coming my way. I scarcely had time to dive behind a statue of Zeus when a short, stocky figure lurched past. I was glad it was the king of the gods I was hiding behind. If it had been a smaller deity I might have been spotted. And that was the last thing I wanted, for the man was Talbot. He was now wrapped in a thick cloak. I set off after him.

As the cold night air of the courtyard hit me, with

only my apron for extra warmth, I cursed Edmund Talbot and his sneakiness.

He headed for the black and white gatehouse that crossed over King Street. He slipped inside, up the stairs and along a shadowy walkway, lit only by the flare of the torches outside.

The other side of the gatehouse led into a large open space with a long decorated fence in the middle. What business could Talbot have in the tiltyard? But he didn't linger. Staggering with drink, he fumbled at the wooden wall. With a grunt of satisfaction he pushed aside a loose board and squeezed out. I followed. We were in King Street. And I was now more convinced than ever that Talbot was up to no good. An honest courtier doesn't leave a feast without permission and then use a secret way out of the palace.

Now we'd left the palace, it was much darker. The sky was black, with no moon or stars to be seen. Talbot swayed and tottered, sometimes heading more sideways than straight. Several people dodged out of his way. I began to wonder if he'd be able to see straight enough to find his destination.

As we passed Charing, it began to rain heavily. It was what old Brother Jerome used to call 'a downpour from the devil's bucket', and I was soon drenched. The ruts in the road became puddles in an instant, sending passers-by scurrying for shelter. My wet livery felt like a coat of ice, but I was glad of the tattoo of raindrops beating on the ground, for they drowned out my footsteps on the cobbles.

We reached a church and Talbot suddenly lurched into a narrow alley beside it.

The church bell struck eight, making me jump. I slipped into the alley and crept along beside the ramshackle walls of closely built houses. The top storeys almost touched, forming a sort of narrow tunnel. Hardly any candles shone through the windows here so I felt my way along, my fingers finding huge gaping holes in the plaster. It felt a million miles from the splendour of the palace. At the very end, a solitary lantern hung over an inn where faint voices were raised in a drunken song. Was Talbot just sneaking off to meet some common drinking companion? After all, he seemed to have no friends at Court.

The stinking alley looked a likely place for thieves or footpads to lurk. And here I was, following a man to who knows where, without even a stick for protection. A noise from a doorway had me whipping round nervously but it was only a cat, streaking across my path.

Ahead of me Talbot stopped and peered around, as if expecting to see someone. A horse and cart came trundling past. Talbot cursed as the cart wheels sent mud splattering all over his cloak.

When the cart had passed, I realised a man stood silhouetted against the glow of the inn. He wore a long cloak like Talbot's and his hat was outlined in fur.

Talbot raised his hand in greeting and the man raised his in return.

Talbot began to weave drunkenly towards him. The man moved impatiently, and I heard the light chink of metal. He was wearing spurs. I had no doubt that this was a gentleman – very likely a courtier. But why were two high-born men meeting in this squalid place? If I was to find out, I had to get closer without being discovered.

The man was standing under a narrow beam that spanned the road, supporting the two houses which leant into each other on either side. From up there I might be able to hear their conversation. I didn't think they'd be expecting an eavesdropper from above.

I pulled myself onto the rotten window ledge behind me, praying that the wood was going to hold. I reached up and grasped a tarred strut that stuck out from the next storey. The crumbling holes in the timber were big enough for my fingers and I hung there for a moment, my feet scrabbling for a foothold on the wall. There was another strut ahead of me. I swung and reached out for it. One more strut and I'd reach the beam above their heads.

I swung again to the next strut. Now I was just over Talbot's head. As the wood took my weight, it let out an almighty creak, juddering as if it would tear itself from the wall. Luckily, Talbot was too busy muttering drunkenly to himself to notice.

'Who goes there?' growled the stranger, starting forward and peering into the gloom.

I froze – as much as someone suspended from a creaking piece of wood *can* freeze. I was in the dark shadows, but if he came forward to investigate and then looked up . . .

'It's only me,' slurred Talbot, from just under my feet. He stumbled and splashed about a bit as he got his balance. 'Coming as you requested, my friend.'

'Then be quick about it,' grunted the man.

My foot found a hole in the plaster and I was able to steady myself. A narrow lump of wood stuck out from under a window just ahead and I crawled onto it. This perch would have to be close enough.

Talbot had finally staggered to the waiting figure. My heart pounded with excitement. What was I about to hear? Treason? I would report every word back to Cromwell.

But there were no words.

As Talbot reached him, the stranger raised his arm and made a jerking movement. Talbot let out a strangled cry and crumpled to the ground. I started forward in surprise and nearly fell off my beam. This didn't look like a greeting between friends. The stranger crouched briefly over Talbot, doing something I couldn't make out. Then he straightened and walked quickly away, moving with a limp. He passed under a beam, nearly dislodging his hat in his haste, and disappeared around the corner of the inn.

Talbot still lay where he'd fallen. If he was unconscious he might be run over by a cart, so I jumped down to pull him out of danger. But as I ran to him, I heard the sudden smack of a whip on a horse's flank and a clatter of hooves coming ahead. I leapt back. The horse flew past, the rider digging his spurs into its flanks, its hooves skidding wildly in the mud. Talbot's assailant had made his getaway.

I bent over Talbot to try to help him. What I saw made me reel in horror. Talbot lay on his back, his eyes wide open but unseeing, his face frozen in a shocked grimace. A huge bloodstain was spreading across his doublet.

The stranger had stabbed him through the heart. Edmund Talbot was dead.

17

I don't know how long I crouched there. I felt I was looking at the sight through cracked glass. It didn't make sense. Talbot had been lured to his death by someone he'd greeted as a friend.

This couldn't wait until Cromwell's return. There was only one other person to confide in – Robert Aycliffe. But what would I be able to tell him about the killer? Very little, except that he had seemed high-born.

Then I remembered the message that Talbot had received. It must have the man's name on. I pulled open the gory jacket. The heavy gold chain gleamed in the faint light. I thrust my hand inside, shuddering as I felt warm, congealing blood, but there was only a purse of coins. The message had gone.

Of course, I thought. *Killers don't like to leave clues.*

I tried to memorise all I could – the stab wound, the

position of Talbot's body, the sword lying in his hand.

The sword in his hand! That was strange. Talbot hadn't had time to draw his sword. There was only one possible explanation. When the killer had leant over him, not only had he taken the message, but he must also have placed Talbot's own sword in his dead fingers.

But why? And as I asked the question, the answer came to me. No one who knew Talbot would be surprised to hear he'd died in a drunken fight. The killer must have thought that by making it look that way he'd committed the perfect murder. But there was one thing he hadn't reckoned with – a witness to his crime.

The faint light from the inn reflected in the puddles and I could see a line of footsteps leading through them, away from the body. They were in the mud of the cart track so they must have been made after the cart went past, and no one else had been down the road since then except Talbot and the man who'd killed him. There was something unusual about the footprints – the right foot had a bulge at the big toe. I knew the sign of a bunion when I saw one. Father Busbrig suffered from bony lumps just like this, and his temper flared whenever they were playing up. I ran my fingers over Talbot's boots. His toes were straight. The peculiar footprint was the murderer's, for certain.

I looked down along the alley the way the murderer had gone and suddenly remembered something else.

When the killer had passed under the beam at the corner it had nearly knocked his hat off. That meant he was about the height of the beam.

I stepped under it and stretched up my arm. I was just able to touch it. Now I knew how tall the murderer was too.

There was nothing more I could do for Talbot, so I raced back to the palace to report to Robert Aycliffe.

∾

The feast was still underway. I slipped in, hoping my absence hadn't been noted.

'What business can a scribe have that cannot wait until the morrow?' Aycliffe said crossly when I suddenly appeared at his shoulder, interrupting him as he took a swig of wine. He looked in astonishment at my soaked clothes. 'A wet scribe, at that!'

'Master Simkins begs a word with you,' I said. 'It's very important.'

I saw a flicker of understanding in Aycliffe's eyes. He pushed back his chair. 'Take me to him and be gone!' This testy remark drew a laugh from his neighbour.

As soon as we were in the passage, his tone changed.

'Master Simkins is proving very useful,' he said with a smile. 'Now, what have you dragged me from my venison for?'

'Edmund Talbot has been murdered,' I said simply.

'God's oath!' exclaimed Aycliffe. 'How do you know?'

'I saw it happen, sir,' I said. 'He left the feast so I followed him.'

'Tell me all!' said Aycliffe.

I told him the night's events. But I think I went into too much detail, for when I began to describe how cleverly I'd tailed my prey, Aycliffe waved an impatient hand. I cut to the moment when Talbot was slain. 'He met a friend,' I finished hurriedly, 'and the friend ran him through. Then he made it look as if Talbot had been fighting.'

'It seems to me that Talbot simply upset one person too many,' said Aycliffe. 'He was notorious for not settling his gambling debts. The killer doubtless took the quick way of getting money from his purse.'

'But his purse and gold chain were still—' I began.

'I see you're keen to prove yourself to our master,' Aycliffe interrupted me, 'but be careful you don't find conspiracy around every corner. The coroner will look at Talbot's death because it happened within the Verge of the Court.' He saw my blank face and smiled. 'The Verge of the Court is a twelve-mile circle around wherever the King is. I'm leaving at dawn for Lutterall House and I'll inform Master Cromwell about the unfortunate death when I arrive. But I suspect he has more important things on his mind at present, preparing for the King's visit. And the French ambassador's kicking up rough at the moment.' He put a hand on my shoulder. 'We follow orders, Jack. I know you were told only to listen to Talbot at the feast. Your job is done.'

'But he left the palace. I had to—'

'You went beyond your instructions,' said Aycliffe. 'That was unwise. You shouldn't have put yourself in danger by following some good-for-nothing around the dark streets. Look, lad, you're new to this and you certainly show promise. Just remember to do as you're told next time.'

I nodded. I was beginning to shiver in my wet clothes.

'Now fetch a dry apron and get back to your serving duties,' Aycliffe told me.

I stood for a long moment, watching him go, thinking over the night's events. Aycliffe had much more experience of such things than I did, and what he'd said about unpaid debts would have made perfect sense – if the killer had taken Talbot's purse and chain. But he hadn't.

I was sure there was some other reason for Talbot's death.

18

I went to sleep with the gruesome image of the dead man's empty stare in my head. I woke early to the sound of a horse's hooves in the courtyard below. I guessed it was Robert Aycliffe leaving for Lutterall House. He would be telling Cromwell about Talbot's death. As far they were concerned, Talbot was nothing but a blabbermouth who was no further threat to the King. Yet I was certain Edmund Talbot had been murdered for something other than gambling debts.

I'd been warned off by Aycliffe and I knew I should heed his warning. But something in me wouldn't let it rest. Brother Matthew would say it was my natural nosiness. I recalled Talbot's shouted words at table. He'd wanted everyone to know that he'd soon become someone to be reckoned with, but Cromwell didn't consider him to be a rising star – and Cromwell knew most things that went on at Court. Was there something my master had missed?

I might discover more about Talbot by searching among his possessions. I guessed they'd still be in his chamber. They might give me a clue to why he'd been murdered, and a clue to his murderer. I resolved to take a look – if I could slip away from the scribes' room and get into Talbot's chamber without arousing suspicion. And I'd find out which servant had delivered the message to him at the feast. The servant would surely remember something about the man who'd given the message to him in the first place.

Oswyn was snoring loudly and there was no sound from Mark so I crept off and took my jacket from the fireside where I'd left it to dry.

'Where are you going?' Mark's sleepy voice made me jump.

'Just off to use the jakes,' I lied. 'Go back to sleep.'

'You don't need to dress for that.'

'Er . . . I'm cold,' I told him, pretending to shiver.

'Are you ailing?' asked Mark in a whisper. 'You shouldn't have gone outside in the rain last night.'

'I told you I didn't mean to,' I assured him, wishing that Mark wasn't quite such a worrier. 'I forgot the way to the kitchen and found myself in the courtyard.'

'Oswyn said you'd been gone an age,' said Mark. 'He's telling everyone you're up to no good. I meant to warn you last night, but I fell asleep before I could.'

'Oswyn's just trying to make trouble,' I said. 'It was

his fault I threw those pies that nearly hit the King!'

Mark sat bolt upright. 'So that was you! I was in the kitchen fetching the partridges when Mr Sorrel came in and told everyone about it. How did it happen?'

Mark obviously wasn't going back to sleep. Talbot's room and the servant would have to wait.

◈

My chance didn't come until late that afternoon. All day the talk in the scribes' room had been of nothing but Talbot's drunken fight and unfortunate death. I already knew that news spread with astonishing speed at the palace. The tales that Oswyn gleaned from around the Court got more and more ridiculous as the day went on. I had to bite my tongue when I heard the man had been set upon by fifty one-armed, cutlass-waving brigands. However, all agreed that he'd been killed in a fight over debts and none seemed sorry.

At last Mister Scrope sent me to deliver a message to the Clerk of the Wine Cellars. The moment my errand was done, I set off to Talbot's chamber. I'd have to be quick. Mister Scrope was expecting me back straightaway. As I approached, I passed a couple of servants talking about the dead man. One held a flagon of beer. The other was leaning on his broom. I stopped to join them, hoping I might hear something interesting.

'Does anyone know who killed Mister Talbot?' I asked.

'Not that I know of,' said Beer Flagon. 'The coroner won't waste much time over a drunken brawl.'

'Too right,' said Broom Man, lowering his voice. 'I for one would shake the man's hand. Talbot was nothing but a clack-dish with his empty words. I'm not sorry he's gone.'

'I heard he got a message last night,' I said in dramatic tones. 'That was why he left the feast.'

'Who was the message from?' asked Beer Flagon.

'You dolt, Samuel,' laughed the man with the broom. 'If we knew that, we'd likely have the name of the man he was fighting! I'd wager my hat that he who summoned him did the deed.'

'Might Talbot's own servant have delivered it?' I asked, hoping for any extra nugget of information. 'If so, he could tell us exactly who gave it to him – and therefore who killed Talbot!'

Samuel Beer Flagon shook his head. 'Talbot got rid of the latest one yesterday morning.'

'I heard he thrashed him first,' put in Broom Man, 'and all because the poor soul went to clean his boots for him! Just doing his duty.'

Here was a motive for murder. Had the servant got his revenge for his ill-treatment? I'd been sure the killer was a gentleman. But if a smock and pig dung could turn me into a swineherd then a cloak, hat and spurs could easily make a servant appear noble. The only thing I knew for certain was the height of the killer – and the bunion. I had no way of asking about the shape of a servant's feet without sounding like a madman.

'I remember Mister Talbot strutting around,' I said, imitating Talbot's chicken walk, 'with a sour-faced servant in tow. It was a ridiculous picture, with the lad so much taller than him.'

'That wouldn't be his servant,' laughed Broom Man. 'He always picked short men to make himself look grand.'

So I was back with my mysterious stranger.

I wished them a good day and walked down the passage. Talbot's room was just ahead, but the men weren't moving. I leant against the door, removed my shoe and pretended to be hunting for a stone inside. At last they ambled off. I shoved my shoe back on and put my ear to the wood, listening hard. There was no sound inside.

I turned the handle, opened the door – and froze. The room was gloomy, lit only by a slit of a window, but a figure was furtively rooting about in a chest by the bed. It was Cat Thimblebee, the horse riding girl. Before I could slip away unseen, she whipped round, her mouth open in horror.

'I'm just putting back a shirt I mended for Mister Talbot, God rest his soul,' she gabbled, trying to push past me. 'That's all.'

I was sure she was lying. She looked sick with guilt.

'If that's the case,' I said, nodding towards the chest,

which was full of nothing but boots, 'where's the shirt?'

'I mended it days ago,' said Cat defiantly, 'but the miserable worm wouldn't pay. I have to give the money to Mister Wiltshire or it will be taken from my wages and it's more than I earn in a year.' The words spilled out in a rush. 'So I thought, seeing as he's dead, he can't complain if I take what's owing and . . .' She suddenly fixed me with a piercing stare. 'Wait a minute! What are *you* doing in here?'

She was well named; she'd turned on me like a spitting cat!

'I'm on business for the Talbot family,' I said, thinking quickly.

The fear flooded over Cat's face again.

'Then you must promise not to tell them what I've done,' she burst out. 'I was within my rights – in a way – but they'll have me branded a thief if you tell!'

'How can I believe you?' I asked. 'You said you're not a rider, but I saw you in the park.'

'I've told you, you're wrong,' hissed Cat. 'It wasn't me on that stallion!'

I grinned. 'Stallion? I never mentioned a stallion.'

'You did,' insisted Cat. 'When you talked all that riding nonsense yesterday.'

'Not me,' I said. 'I wouldn't know a stallion from a starling!'

'But . . .' For once the girl didn't seem to have an answer.

'I won't tell anyone what you've been up to . . .' I began.

'Oh yes,' said Cat, scornfully. 'And what do you want in return?'

I was about to say 'nothing' but changed my mind.

'There *is* one thing,' I said.

'Go on,' muttered Cat.

'Teach me to ride.'

Cat's eyes widened in surprise.

'I really need to learn.'

'I can't,' said Cat. 'I shouldn't be riding myself.'

'Then I'll have to keep the secret too,' I assured her, 'or we'll both be in trouble.'

Cat was quiet for a moment. 'And you'll let me take the money for the mending back to Mister Wiltshire?'

'Of course,' I said. 'Talbot's family would want all debts paid.'

Without another word, Cat searched feverishly among the dead man's possessions. At last she found a small purse in a leather bag, counted out some money and placed the purse back. 'Tell them I've only taken what's owing,' she insisted as she hurried to the door, 'and not a penny more.'

'Wait!' I called after her. 'What about my riding lesson?'

'Lesson?' said Cat incredulously. 'What are you talking about?'

'You can't break your promise.'

'I'm not going to,' said Cat. 'But you must be mazed

101

to think you'll only want one.' She looked me up and down. 'A hundred, more like. But I've agreed to teach you, so I shall. Meet me tomorrow morning at six o'clock under the dead elm in St James's Park. Just don't let anyone see you.'

19

Cat slipped off. I punched the air. At last I was going to learn to ride. Whatever she said, it wouldn't take me long to master the art. There'd be no more pretending to have boils on my bum.

But now I had to concentrate on Edmund Talbot. Where should I start to look for clues to his murder? Perhaps in the days before his death he'd received other messages from his killer – a man Talbot considered a friend, judging by the way he'd greeted him last night.

There was nothing among the clothes scattered on the bed and shoes strewn all over the floor, although I searched them all thoroughly. The table in the corner only provided a collection of empty wine pitchers and a couple of goblets.

I felt under the bed, coughing in the dust. The first thing I pulled out was a chamber pot that sloshed as I moved it, then a bootjack and some blankets. I gave the blankets a shake but all I found were dead moths. I put everything back carefully – even the moths!

Now I'd searched every place where a message was likely to have been stored – or, more likely, tossed down carelessly by this untidy man. I cursed Talbot for not keeping his latest servant. It would have made my job much easier if the room had been in order. The men in the passageway had told me that Talbot's servant had been whipped and dismissed just because he'd wanted to clean his master's boots.

Why wouldn't you let your servant near your boots? It was madness. I stared inside the boot chest again. The boots reeked of stinking feet and stale horse dung. They were in dire need of a clean. It would have been the first job I'd have given a servant. Unless . . . unless there was something in them I didn't want anyone to see!

I plunged my hand into each boot, keeping my nose from the smell, and tossed them onto the bed next to me when I was finished. Finally there was only one boot left, lying flat at the very bottom of the chest. Not daring to hope now, I felt inside . . .

God's teeth! There was something, rammed into the toe! I pulled out a piece of parchment and unfolded it. It was a letter.

The writing was scrawling and uneven and there was a red-wine stain on one corner. The letter tailed off at the end, with no signature. This was obviously not written *to* Talbot. It was one he'd written himself and never sent. *What can this half-written drunken scribble possibly tell me about Talbot's fate?* I thought.

I threw the boots back into the chest and was about to stick the letter in with them when I remembered Cromwell's words: *Even if it seems trivial to you, I will require all the details.*

I read the letter again, by the light of the window, struggling to make sense of the writing.

'*My dear friend,*' it began. '*You have stayed away from Court like a coward while I have been working ceaselessly. You seem to have no notion of what is involved in bringing about the success of our cause.*'

This sounded serious. I read on.

'*It requires the utmost toil and the utmost secrecy to avoid arousing suspicion and to ensure our plans only reach the ears of those loyal to our purpose.*'

It took me a while to make out the last line. '*There are many here who want to help bring justice for the wrongly and unfairly treated Pr . . .*'

Here a long splatter of ink trailed away across the page. Talbot must have been too drunk to continue and then, when he was sober, realised that his words could incriminate him, so he'd hidden the letter, meaning to finish it at another time. Its meaning was evident. Talbot had not just been an idle clack-dish. He'd been deeply involved in a secret plan to bring justice to someone whose name began with *Pr.*

Cromwell needed to see the letter.

I heard footsteps outside the door. The door handle

began to turn. I hastily stuffed the letter up my sleeve, stood on the chest and climbed up to the window. I was faced with a sheer drop and no helpful scaffolding. The bed was my only hiding place. I threw myself under it and pulled the chamber pot and blankets in front of me. I cursed myself for being so stupid. Next time I was ferreting around in someone's chamber I'd plan my exit first.

I saw a man walk in. At least, I saw his feet. They went right past the bed. It was soon clear what he was doing. Like me, he was searching Talbot's chamber. Boots came flying out of the chest. He picked up the clothes and pillows from the floor and quickly discarded them. I heard clunks and scrapes as the pitchers were moved about on the table.

Who else would want to search Talbot's room? I wondered. One of his family? Had Robert Aycliffe decided there was more to Talbot's death after all and changed his mind about going to Lutterall House? Or was Cromwell taking the murder seriously and had sent someone to investigate? Questions whirred through my brain.

The searcher was standing close to the bed now and I saw something that almost made me cry out in shock. The leather of one of his boots bulged out in a lump by the big toe. The man had a bunion – on his right foot.

I was inches away from Talbot's killer.

My heart pounded painfully. I tried to steady my breathing. It would be one thing to be found by one of

Cromwell's men – but to be discovered by a murderer! I fought down my feeling of panic. I had to concentrate.

A hand appeared, feeling between the mattress and the ropes it lay on.

What was the man looking for? Could he be involved in Talbot's plot too? If so, why suddenly kill a collaborator?

The only evidence I'd found was the letter and I had that safe. I quickly felt in my sleeve to be sure. It wasn't there! It must have dropped out as I'd hurried to hide. I cursed inwardly. Something pale was wedged between the chest and the wall.

The intruder moved away towards the table. I stretched out my hand to try and reach the letter. But my knuckles knocked against the chamber pot. For a brief moment I thought the man hadn't heard the sound. But then he stopped and turned. In a second he'd dropped to his knees by the bed. He grasped the blankets and pulled them out, knocking the chamber pot over. The smell of stale piss nearly choked me. Now his fingers were feeling round across the floorboards. I shrank back against the wall, thankful for the shadows that hid me. The fingers stopped just short of my nose.

The arm withdrew.

I heard a cold sliding sound. The sound of a sword being pulled slowly from its scabbard.

The blade caught the light as it flashed along the floor towards me. It struck the wall by my head and then withdrew – ready to strike again.

20

I reached for the ropes strapped across the bed frame. Hooking my feet into them, I pulled myself clear of the ground.

The murderer's sword scraped across the floor, to and fro, then lunged into the furthest corners. My face was pressed hard against the ropes and every muscle was screaming for me to let go.

My fingers began to lose their grip and my whole body shook with the effort of keeping away from the deadly blade. Dust swirled round my face. Suddenly I felt I was going to sneeze. I held my breath and pressed my nose into the mattress. I knew that, if I gave in, it would be the last thing I ever did.

Now there was silence. I heard the sword withdraw and the feet move away from the bed. Arms trembling, I lowered myself to the floor.

The man marched back and forth across the room.

'There must be something!' he whispered, giving the chest an angry kick. My heart sank as I heard the soft swish of the letter falling to the floor. The man had heard it too. In an instant he'd pulled aside the chest and I saw his hand snatch it up. I could imagine him examining the scrawled handwriting.

He moved towards the fireplace. I heard the sharp striking of flint on a tinderbox and smelt burning. Small lumps of ash fell into the grate like black snowflakes.

Then the man was gone. I lay for long minutes, dreading that he might return. Finally I dragged myself out from under the bed.

I rooted among the cinders, hoping that part of the writing had escaped the flames. I found nothing but the corner with the wine stain. I cursed. There was some plot festering away at Court like a beggar's sore and now I had no evidence of it.

And the coroner was likely to put Talbot's murder down to a drunken brawl, as Aycliffe had. I was the only one in the entire Court who knew that a conspiracy had led to Talbot's death.

As I ran back to the scribes' chamber I thought about what my next move should be.

My one link to the conspiracy was the murderer.

So I decided that my next task would be to find out his name. I listed in my head what I knew about him. He was a tall, high-born gentleman with a bunion, and he must be a courtier or he wouldn't be free to walk around the palace. It wasn't much to go on.

According to Mark, there were hundreds of courtiers here at Whitehall. But if I tracked down the servant who'd delivered the note to Talbot, I might hear some valuable information about the sender that would help me identify him. I guessed that work in the scribes' office must be nearly finished for the day, so I'd be free to carry on my search.

'What have you to say for yourself, Jack Briars?' demanded Mister Scrope angrily as I slipped into the office. 'You could have walked to the wine cellars at Greenwich in the time you've been away!'

'I got lost,' I told him quickly. 'I'm not used to the palace yet. I got to the buttery and I turned right instead of left and I ended up in the wood yard and that got me completely confused and—'

'Spare me the details,' Mister Scrope interrupted. 'Get extra candles out of the chest. We've got hours more work to do tonight.'

'Master Cromwell sent word that he wants copies of his correspondence with the French Ambassador,' Mark explained as he brought a pile of documents to our table. 'It's to be sent to Lutterall House when the Court goes there tomorrow.'

My master had unwittingly thrown a huge boulder in my path.

'We'll be here until midnight!' complained Oswyn, 'seeing as you've been shirking.'

Once we'd started the work, Mark leant over, an excited look on his face.

'I know something Oswyn doesn't,' he whispered. 'It's about Talbot's death.'

I stopped writing. 'What is it?' I tried not to sound too eager.

'I heard that before Talbot was killed he got a message from the killer! And Joe in the bakehouse saw him.'

'Joe saw the killer?'

'Well, he didn't exactly see him,' admitted Mark. 'He found a sealed letter under one of his loaves that was cooling, ready for the feast, and the letter had Edmund Talbot's name on it. So he took it to the door of the Presence Chamber but he didn't dare go in, so he gave it to Hubert who was serving at table. And Hubert delivered it!'

'Shame Joe didn't see who put the letter under the loaf,' I said. 'He could have come face to face with the culprit himself.'

'That's not a shame.' Mark looked horrified. 'That's a blessing. If you're right, Joe had a narrow escape.' He was probably picturing poor Joe being run through in the bakehouse.

'Didn't anyone else see who it was?' I asked. 'There must have been plenty of people around.'

Mark shook his head. 'Joe said they were all too busy at their ovens.'

'Less talking and more copying,' called Mister Scrope, stuffing a sweetmeat into his mouth.

I went back to my work. As I copied the flowery greetings from the French Ambassador – in English, thank goodness – I knew I was back to searching for the tall, bunioned man. But by the time we finished with Jean de Dinteville and his messages from King Francis, his monarch, there'd be no chance of finding him tonight. Tonight I was penned in by the pen!

21

As the sun rose next morning I dashed across King Street and into St James's Park for my riding lesson. The bells were ringing six all over London. The dead elm stood stark against the lightening sky and I made straight for it and leant against it, yawning. We'd finally been allowed to go to bed at two o'clock, but I was glad the lesson was so early – the courtiers wouldn't be up so I couldn't go on with my search for Talbot's killer yet.

I looked round for a galloping seamstress. The park was deserted. I wondered if Cat had sent me here as a joke. As I waited, my breath making clouds in the cold air, the mystery of Talbot's death filled my mind. How was I going to find his killer? I couldn't lean out of the office window and shout for every courtier with a bunion to report to me. And I'd be sure to be noticed if I crawled about under the breakfast tables, checking all

113

the high-born feet. Anyway, what excuse would I have to leave the scribes' room this time? Mister Scrope wouldn't put up with me popping off and reappearing hours later. I certainly didn't want to lose my job.

I heard the thundering of hooves. A huge black horse came charging up, with Cat in the saddle. It was the stallion I'd seen before. She waved to me, holding the reins loosely in her other hand, and charged away among the trees. Horse and rider vanished, though I could still hear the hoofbeats.

'Show-off!' I muttered.

The horse trotted back into view. There was no one in the saddle! I ran under the trees, expecting to find a crumpled heap with a broken neck.

'Cat!' I yelled. 'Cat, are you hurt?'

A cackle of laughter rang out above my head and she appeared, hanging upside down, her bright red curls escaping from her cap like a waterfall. She clicked her tongue. The horse trotted up until it was immediately below her and stayed there calmly while she flipped from the branch and landed in the saddle.

'What do you think of my trick?' she asked, patting the horse's gleaming neck. 'I've been practising it.'

'Very clever,' I said sarcastically. Secretly I was impressed. The Court tumblers couldn't have bettered it, but I wasn't going to give her the satisfaction of hearing that.

'What am I riding?' I demanded, looking round for a nice safe old pony.

Cat leapt from the saddle. 'Diablo here, of course.'

'I can't ride him; he's huge and wild!' I gasped. I didn't add that the name was enough to put me off. He truly looked like a devil horse.

'Don't be a dunderhead,' said Cat scornfully. 'He'll be no trouble. Diablo's a sweetheart.' She rubbed the stallion's nose. I waited for Diablo to bite her but he just nuzzled her cheek. 'He's the King's horse,' she went on.

'You're riding the King's horse!' I spluttered. 'Are you mad?'

'How ungrateful,' said Cat. 'I've brought you the best horse in the stable.'

'But . . .' I began.

'Don't worry,' said Cat soothingly. 'King Henry doesn't ride him any more. Diablo was a present from Queen Katherine, so Henry shuns the poor thing now.'

She produced an apple from her apron pocket and Diablo chomped down on it hard.

'He needs a lot of exercise,' she went on. 'So I take him out whenever I can – secretly, of course. The stablehands turn a blind eye, glad to have Diablo given a good run. It was just bad luck that you spotted me the other evening. I'm usually so careful,' her eyes flashed. 'But I couldn't resist galloping up that hill and Diablo wanted to as well. Anyway, what are we wasting time for? Let's get you on board.'

She bent down and cupped her hands. 'Stick your foot in here and I'll hoist you up.'

She expected me to back away. Well, she was wrong. I did as she'd instructed and found myself bundled into the saddle. The ground seemed a long way away – and that from a boy who'd been clambering about high up on the palace! But then the palace hadn't tossed its head and stamped its hooves.

Cat grasped my feet and set them firmly in the long, flat stirrups. She showed me how to hold the reins. I'd rather have clung to the sturdy-looking lump on the front of the saddle but I knew she'd laugh at me.

She took the bridle and clicked her tongue. Diablo moved forwards and instinctively I clamped my legs tightly to his flanks. The horse gave a skip and I clamped even tighter.

'Relax!' called Cat, pulling Diablo to a halt. 'If you squeeze like that he thinks you want to be off!' She threw me a challenging look. 'Or perhaps you do?'

'Maybe not today,' I said, trying to sound casual.

'First things first. How to make your horse walk and not think it's in a race,' Cat began.

She told me to squeeze my legs gently and relax the reins. Diablo immediately began to walk. The saddle, which curved up in front and behind, began to make me feel safe.

'That was simple,' I said. 'Can I go a bit faster now?'

'Not before you've learnt how to stop,' laughed Cat. 'Straighten your back and tighten the reins a little.'

I obeyed. Well, I thought I did. Diablo stopped abruptly.

'Don't pull!' exclaimed Cat. 'You'll hurt his poor mouth. He's not an old nag. He only needs a light touch.'

I practised starting and stopping with Cat by Diablo's side.

'*Now* can we go a bit faster?' I asked as we ambled along.

'Not yet,' replied Cat. 'First you've got to prove you can control Diablo yourself. Bring him to a halt.' She walked off a short distance. 'Now make him walk to me,' she said.

'Easy,' I said. I squeezed the stallion's flanks with my legs. Nothing happened. I squeezed a little harder. Still nothing. The third time I tried, Diablo bent down and started eating the grass.

'He knows you're not in charge,' said Cat smugly. She came over and touched Diablo on the flank. The stallion moved forwards obediently. I was irritated that this beast took no notice of me, while an annoying little seamstress could make him do whatever she wanted.

'I soon will be,' I said through gritted teeth. Cat chuckled under her breath. This wasn't exactly the picture I'd had of myself, galloping wildly over open country. I wanted to feel what it was like to really move! 'Come on, let me go a bit faster,' I urged again. 'I'll be all right.'

I felt a sudden jolt, let go of the reins and nearly fell backwards over the horse's rear.

Cat snorted with laughter. 'Now we're trotting,' she told me as I clutched wildly at the horse's mane. 'You'll find that Diablo has a very comfortable trot.'

'It might be . . . comfortable for Diablo,' I panted, 'but it's . . . not for me.' The words came out in short jerks.

Cat took no notice but carried on running over the grass, with Diablo trotting beside her. I fumbled for the reins.

'Hold the saddle if you're scared,' said Cat airily.

'Scared?' I managed to answer. 'Not me.'

'That's just what my brothers used to say!' exclaimed Cat. 'They never rode as well as I did, although we all had equal goes on Bessie. She was the old nag in the field by our cottage. Not that Bessie's owner knew anything about our antics.' She rattled on about her six brothers and I tried to listen over the sound of my teeth rattling in my head.

At last the chapel clock in the distance chimed the half hour. Cat immediately brought Diablo to a halt.

'Lesson over,' she told me. 'I have work to do, even if you don't.'

Every muscle in my body felt as if it had been battered with a club, but I'd had my first ride without falling off! Soon, Cat wouldn't be making fun of me, she'd be racing to catch up with me! Hoping to look like an expert, I swung my leg over the saddle to dismount. My other foot caught in the stirrup and I fell to the frosty ground on my bum. I scrambled to my feet, trying to ignore Cat's chortles. Diablo whinnied and snorted loudly, sending clouds of oaty steam into my face. Now even the horse was laughing at me!

'Thank you for the lesson,' I said, straightening my cap, 'but in future I shall find a different teacher – one who doesn't mock my efforts.' I turned to go. Of course, I had no intention of finding another teacher but I wasn't going to tell her that.

'Wait!' said Cat. 'I've something to ask you.' She hooked Diablo's reins round her arm. The devil horse nuzzled her ear.

I stopped. 'You'd better ask it quickly for I also have work to do.'

'Why were you really in that room yesterday?'

'I've told you already,' I began.

'You told me something,' said Cat, 'but it turned out to be mere flimflam.'

I looked at her. My heartbeat quickened. What did she know?

'You weren't acting for the family at all!' she exclaimed. 'I heard they've sent their own servants because they didn't want anyone at the palace touching Talbot's belongings.' She looked at me defiantly. 'I told you the truth – now you can repay the favour.'

22

The tables had turned. But I couldn't tell Cat the real reason I'd been in Talbot's chamber. I tried to think calmly.

'I was passing and I heard a noise,' I tried.

'Why didn't you say that in the first place?' demanded Cat.

'Well . . .' I began, wishing I *had* said it in the first place.

'That's a lie too, isn't it?' persisted Cat. 'You sneaked in just like I did and I want to know why.' She stared at me fiercely. 'And I'll set Diablo on you if you don't tell me.'

I knew she wouldn't. She'd be too worried her precious horse would get hurt. But she might refuse to give me any more riding lessons.

Cromwell had said I mustn't speak of my extra duties to anyone. But Master Cromwell had never told me to investigate Talbot's death. That was all my idea.

'Edmund Talbot was murdered and I want to know who did it,' I told her.

'Murdered?' gasped Cat. 'You're wrong. Everyone knows it was just a fight over debts.'

'It was a cold-blooded killing,' I went on. 'I saw it. And I intend to track down the killer.'

'Aren't you going to tell the coroner?' asked Cat, incredulous.

I shook my head. 'No one believes it was murder. I need proof before anyone will listen.'

'I'm listening,' said Cat.

So I told her, but I left out any mention of Master Cromwell. It was a relief to share my secret.

'What made you follow Talbot in the first place?' exclaimed Cat, when I'd finished.

Another awkward question.

'I . . . had a feeling about him. And it turns out I was right.'

'And now he's dead,' said Cat, thoughtfully stoking Diablo's nose. 'Killed by a tall man with a bunion on his right foot that makes him limp and who's definitely a courtier and who could still be at the palace. That's what you said, isn't it?'

'Yes,' I said, 'but it's not easy to search for him. I can't leave the scribes' room whenever I want.'

'I'll find him for you,' said Cat confidently. 'I'm always running about the palace for Mr Wiltshire.'

She was right. No one would take any notice of a

seamstress with an armful of linen. And I was about to tell her yes, but my conscience stopped me. I might be putting her in great danger. Was this how Cromwell felt when he sent spies out to do perilous work? Or had he learnt to be ruthless, putting King and country before the lives of his men?

'This is different,' I said, reluctantly. 'We're not talking about mended breeches. You'll be tracking a murderer. It's not safe.'

'Try and stop me,' said Cat.

'But . . .'

'I'm not going to go up to him and say, *Excuse me, did you kill Mr Talbot, by any chance?*'

'I know, but . . .'

'I'll simply go about my work and no one will know I've got my eyes on them.'

My conscience told me to have one last try.

'The King and the Court are leaving this morning for Lutterall House and the man I'm looking for is probably going too,' I said lamely. 'So there won't be enough time.'

'I'll start straight away,' said Cat decidedly.

I gave up. The girl was unstoppable! 'Remember – the bunion's on his right foot and he's this tall.' I stretched my hand up above my head, to show the height of the beam the man had passed under on the night he'd killed Talbot.

Cat reached up. On tiptoes she could just touch my fingers with hers. 'I'll find him.'

'Take care,' I warned her. 'This man is dangerous.'

Cat's expression was briefly scornful again. 'I'm not a clodpole!' she snorted, as she took hold of Diablo's stirrup.

'How will you get news to me?' I asked.

'This afternoon I shall be in the little sewing room next to the laundry,' said Cat. 'We have to check all the linen once the Court's gone, so you might have to dig me out from under a great big pile of sheets. I should have a name for you then.' She grinned as she swung herself into Diablo's saddle. 'And, by the way, you'll need plenty more riding tuition, that's certain. You looked like a sack of turnips.'

My brain whirred for a retort to give the abominable girl but Diablo reared and galloped off, showering me with mud.

Gritting my teeth, I made my way back to the palace.

The next time we met, *I'd* be the one who got the last word!

23

I'd barely stepped into the scribes' chamber when Oswyn left his copying and blocked my path. He had a smile on his face but he looked as friendly as a wolf greeting a tasty sheep.

'I've been biding my time,' he hissed. He tapped his nose with his finger. I was pleased to see he left a big ink smudge there. 'This is the first chance I've had to speak to you on the quiet. Scrope's stuffing his gob and Helston won't interfere.'

'Interfere with what?' I asked.

'Our little bit of business. I saw you disappearing from the feast the other night. Master Cromwell would be interested to hear that.'

'Disappearing?' I said pleasantly, but my stomach tightened. 'Surely you saw me chatting to His Majesty! You introduced us, after all.'

Oswyn turned red with rage. 'I mean later, you dolt!'

I shrugged. 'I went to get bread when I was ordered to, if that's what you mean.' I pretended I wasn't worried. 'What will Master Cromwell say when you tell him that, Oswyn? Will he lock me in the Tower, do you think?'

Weasel-face prodded me in the chest. 'Why have you got this job?' he growled. 'My brother was next in line for a position here. Master Cromwell said there were no places, yet suddenly here you are. It's not fair. We're a well-connected family and don't expect to have urchins pushing in front of us. You won't last long. I'll make sure of that.'

I tried not to show that I was really worried now. I *had* left the feast without permission and Weasel-face had seen me go. That had been careless. I decided to strike back.

'Mister Scrope,' I called. 'Would you like me to wipe Oswyn's nose for him?'

The Chief Scribe raised his head from his plate of cheat bread and eels.

'He has a smudge, right there,' I went on. I dabbed the spot of ink on Oswyn's nose.

Oswyn swung his fist, but I hadn't lived for twelve years with a vicious abbot without learning a thing or two. I dodged the blow.

'Oswyn Drage!' said Mister Scrope, spitting crumbs everywhere. 'Jack's right. There's ink all over your nose. Clean yourself up.'

Muttering, Oswyn rubbed at the ink with a rag. We

all returned to work. Mark gave me a wink. He must have enjoyed seeing the bully receive his just reward for once.

At last the chapel bells struck two o'clock. I wondered how Cat was getting on. I hoped she'd been careful. Seeing her ride that huge black beast was proof that she was willing to tackle anything, but did it also mean she was foolhardy? Whatever had happened, I had to know.

Mister Scrope was bent over a parchment. The man hadn't eaten anything for at least twenty minutes. I went to stand respectfully by his side.

'Yes?' he asked without looking up.

'I fear you must be very hungry, sir,' I said. 'Shall I get you something from the kitchen?'

Scrope put down his pen and looked at me suspiciously.

'They're making rabbit pies,' I went on, inventing madly. 'Tom the log boy told me that a trader brought in a sack full of coneys and they'll be cooked in white sauce and . . .'

'Fetch me one,' said Scrope, licking his lips.

I left. I'd have to think up some pie disaster to explain to Mister Scrope why I was coming back empty-handed.

&

I pushed open the door of the little sewing room. Two lads sat by a great pile of folded sheets, stitching the hem of a velvet cloak from each end. Mister Wiltshire was holding an ornate bodice up to the window to inspect the embroidery. There was no sign of Cat.

'Where's Cat Thimblebee?' I said, realising my voice had come out in an anxious squeak.

They all looked up in surprise.

'Who wants me?'

A mass of red hair appeared from behind the sheets. I grinned in relief.

Cat stared back at me as if I was a complete stranger.

'Yes?' she said. Her voice was cool and unfriendly. 'What do you want?'

I was completely taken aback. This girl blew hot and cold!

'Er . . . Mister Scrope in the scribes' office said my shirt cuffs were a disgrace,' I gabbled, 'and I should ask someone to mend them.'

I stretched out an arm and showed her my ragged cuff. 'It's a bit dark in here,' I burbled on. 'I'll show you outside in the light.'

'I work for the nobles of the Court,' said Cat with a sniff, 'not the riff-raff.'

The two lads laughed.

Mister Wiltshire glared at them and they fell upon their sewing at once. Then he seemed to take pity on me. 'Maybe when we're not so busy, lad,' he said. He looked down at my wrists. 'Though there's precious little left to mend.'

I had no choice but to turn and leave.

'Jack!' came a whispered voice behind me.

I spun round to see Cat hurrying along the passageway towards me, a big grin on her face. 'My acting was good, wasn't it?' she said. 'No one would have guessed what I was up to.'

I felt a complete fool. I hadn't guessed either!

'I haven't got long,' Cat went on. 'Mister Wiltshire believes I've gone for some lavender to make herb pillows.'

She bundled me through a door into a small courtyard next to a smelly compost heap.

'There's no one around,' she said. 'Now we can talk about our murder investigation.'

The girl seemed to think we were equal partners! I was about to retort that it was *my* murder investigation and she was just helping out, but her next words made me forget all about it.

'I have news,' she said triumphantly. 'I've found the killer.'

24

'**Y**ou've found the killer!' I exclaimed. 'Who is it?'

Cat held up a hand. 'Not so fast,' she said annoyingly. 'I'll tell you how it happened. I started close to the Court Gate. There were courtiers everywhere with their servants staggering behind loaded with chests and such – all off to Lutterall House, and all in a panic, for the King was about to leave and some of them weren't ready. It makes me laugh when they go visiting. They take more garments than we'll own in a lifetime!'

'And did you find the man there?' I was getting impatient and Cat knew it. She was spinning out her tale.

'No,' she said, 'though I stretched my hand up behind every tall gentleman. One of them turned to me so I quickly pretended to be pointing. Soon the whole courtyard was wondering what was so interesting on the roof! It was funny!'

'This is all very fascinating,' I began, 'but . . .'

'Be patient,' said Cat. 'I never knew how many men were afflicted with bunions at Whitehall. I had a business finding the right one. Well, I couldn't see the man there so I thought that if he's a courtier and going with the King then he might still be on his way to the courtyard. Anyway, as I was going around, delivering muslin bags to the spicery by the longest way, my eyes everywhere so I didn't miss anything, I spotted the bunion – well, I could hardly miss it. It put all the others in the shade. It was so big I nearly fell over it. Its owner is a gentleman and he's really tall! I followed him and managed to check his height.'

'How?' Although I was desperate for her to give me his name, I found myself wanting to know how she'd done it.

'It was easy,' said Cat loftily. 'I noticed which brick his head came up to when he walked by a wall. Then I stretched up to see if it was the same as the height you'd told me. I was so excited when I found it was. A few people looked at me strangely. I think they thought I was trying to climb the wall.'

'So what was the man's name?' I asked.

'All in good time,' said Cat. 'Luckily Simon Tovell came by – he works in the dairy – and I asked him whether the tall man was Sir Charles Fairbrass. I said I'd got his mending and didn't want to miss him as he'd soon be off with His Majesty. I know exactly who Sir Charles Fairbrass is, of course, but I just pretended I didn't – you understand?'

I understood. I just wished she'd finish her story.

'Simon said how could a lanky gentleman like that be Fairbrass – Sir Charles is as small as a child and I must be a silly lass for making that mistake. Then he told me the name of the man I'd pointed out.'

She puffed herself up. 'And then I was really clever. I said, "Of course I know him. His chamber is next to the Duke of Norfolk's" and Simon said, "You addlewit. Of course it's not. It's on the first floor, two doors down from the main staircase – river end."' Cat stopped, a broad smile on her face. 'You must admit – I did a good job!'

'I will – when you tell me *who he is*!' I said desperately.

'His name is Hugh Harrington,' said Cat. 'See, I've sorted it out for you.'

'Thank you,' I forced myself to say.

'Shall we have him arrested?' asked Cat eagerly.

'We have no evidence,' I said. 'Only what I saw – and no one will believe me against a courtier. We have to find a link between Edmund Talbot, Hugh Harrington and someone whose name begins with Pr.' I suddenly realised what I'd said. '*I* have to, I mean.'

'No, you were right the first time,' said Cat. 'You need my help. Let me think.' Her forehead creased in a frown, then she shook her head. 'I've been at

Court a long time, but those names mean nothing to me.'

'Leave it to me,' I said firmly. 'The man will have gone with the King by now, so there's nothing more to be done at the moment.'

'That's where you're wrong,' said Cat. 'He hasn't gone – not yet, anyway. Simon said it was a shame I wasn't trying to return mending to Mister Harrington because he wasn't going to leave Court for Lutterall House until this evening.'

This was interesting.

'Then I know exactly what to do next,' I said.

'What's that?' asked Cat.

'I can't tell you,' I said mysteriously. 'It's something I have to do myself.'

For once I'd got the last word. Or so I thought.

'Well, you know where to find me when you have your next setback,' said Cat.

'I'll remember that,' I said grimly. 'But for now I must be on my way.'

'Before you go,' Cat grinned cheekily, 'have you found someone else to be your riding tutor? I'm sure they're queuing up to teach a sack of turnips to ride one of the King's horses.'

'All the finest horsemen are at Lutterall House,' I said with a careless shrug. 'I'll make do with you for the moment.'

'If you insist,' said Cat, sighing dramatically. 'I think I can fit you in at six tonight. Don't be late.'

She hurried off. I should have been grateful to her. She'd got me the name of the murderer. But the rest was my business and it wasn't going to be hers. I wondered if all girls chattered endlessly like her. There hadn't been any at the abbey for me to find out. Anyway, my next step must be taken very carefully. Cat had been clever getting the information from the servant – not that I was going to tell her that – but I would take a leaf from her book. I'd speak to Harrington's servant and see if I could find out something useful. Like, why was Harrington going to Lutterall House so much later than the other courtiers?

One thing was certain. I'd have to be clever with my questions or the servant would go straight to his master and tell him about the nosy scribe. Harrington had already killed once to keep his business secret.

I was sure he would do so again.

25

Harrington's chamber was closer to the King's apartments than Talbot's – Mister Harrington was clearly a more important courtier than his victim had been. I walked along the passageway, dodging the armies of workers who seemed to be cleaning every tapestry and statue in the palace. All the rooms I passed were empty. Their noble occupants had gone off with the King. I found a miserable-looking fellow scrubbing the floor of Harrington's chamber and muttering into his beard. This must be one of the palace servants. God's teeth! My quarry had gone!

'Excuse me,' I said politely, making him jump out of his skin. 'Is Mister Harrington about?'

The servant wiped his hands on his apron. 'There's no knowing where my master is these days,' he said. So this *was* Harrington's servant. I was surprised. Courtiers' servants didn't usually do the cleaning.

'He's somewhere in the palace, I've no doubt, but he won't be coming back to his chamber.' He waved his hand over the wet floorboards. 'Not with all this going on. Is there a message for him?'

I shook my head. 'You might be able to help,' I said, thinking quickly. 'In Master Cromwell's office there's a list of those lodging at Lutterall House tomorrow. Mister Harrington's name seemed to have been missed off, so I've come to check that he will be among the guests.'

'He'll be there all right,' said the servant grumpily. 'And so should I be, but I'm ordered to stay behind, would you believe it?'

'You're not going with him?' I asked, as if I was shocked.

'No, I'm not!' retorted the man. 'He tells me today that he wants me to look to his room, as it's in a terrible state and very smelly, and it'll want more than a day's cleaning and I'm the only one who can do it properly for him! It's not that bad, and I don't see why it should be me all of a sudden – the palace servants have always done it before and he's never complained – but suddenly he's turned into a right fusspot.'

'Very strange.' I agreed. I was intrigued. Why wouldn't Harrington want his servant with him at Lutterall House? The servant was obviously aggrieved by this. Perhaps that would make him more talkative. 'He could at least have told you why he's not taking you with him,' I said.

'You'd think so,' said the servant, 'but no. He *says* he's to see his lawyer in Chelsea tonight and stay in lodgings there and then on to Lutterall House at first light. A fine courtier he'll look in the King's presence if he has no servant to sort out his clothes and such!'

'Maybe he's travelling with a friend and will make use of their servant,' I said, hoping to hear a name of a possible conspirator.

'Not that he's told me,' grumbled the man. He began scrubbing again. 'I wonder if his mind's disturbed.'

'Why would you say that?' I asked.

'Well, he's told me a lot of nonsense lately. For one thing, his lawyer doesn't live in Chelsea and, for another, he's not ordered me to tell the stables to make his horse ready like he usually does!'

So Harrington was lying, I thought. He was going somewhere secret and didn't want anyone following. Well, he was going to be unlucky tonight.

The servant suddenly looked at me, worried. 'Here, you won't tell him I think he's mazed, will you?'

'Of course not,' I said sympathetically as I turned to go. 'And, if you see your master, don't tell him about the Lutterall House list. It might disturb his mind even more if he thinks he was left off it!'

'Indeed I won't!' said the man with a grim laugh.

'Peter!' We both jumped.

'My master!' whispered the servant in alarm.

A tall man limped into the room. So this was Hugh Harrington! I dipped my head respectfully, hoping he wouldn't see the shock on my face. I felt his eyes on me. Was he wondering what I was doing there? My gaze was drawn to his sword. I'd escaped it once. I hoped I wouldn't have to again. To my huge relief, he began to talk to his man. I risked a look. Harrington towered over us. I recognised the fur-trimmed hat that he'd worn on the night he'd killed Talbot.

Suddenly he turned to me. 'Are you here to help Peter?' he asked. 'I've given him rather a lot to do.'

I'd never met a murderer before, and it was a great surprise to find him quite ordinary – friendly, even. How could such a man be a killer? And yet he was. The thought of the blood on his hands made me turn cold.

'No, sir,' I gabbled, lowering my head again in a sort of bow. I didn't want him to remember too much about me and I didn't want to get stuck cleaning the room. 'I just brought Peter some soap.'

And I left! I clattered down the passage so that he'd hear my departure. Then I crept back and listened at the door.

'Are you sure you won't be needing your horse, master?' asked Peter.

'Not tonight,' said Harrington. 'It'll be the river for me. Now, where are my gloves?'

I heard a chest being opened.

'Here, sir,' came Peter's voice. Footsteps were coming towards the door. This time I really did run!

When I was out of sight, I slowed to a walk. Tonight

I would be following a man who'd murdered and might kill again. I remembered Brother Matthew's words as I'd left the abbey – *Just stay out of trouble*. I tried not to think about how my godfather would feel if anything happened to me. Did I owe it to him to give up my investigation?

But I'd never given up in my life – even at the abbey when Father Busbrig had beaten me till I fell to the ground. I was going to get to the bottom of this. I didn't know how deep this plot went, but it had to be important for a man to have been killed for it.

I hurried back to work and tried in vain to slip into my seat unnoticed.

'Where have you been, boy?' Mister Scrope was glaring at me. 'And where's my pie?'

I'd forgotten all about the pie – and I had no excuse for being away so long. 'There weren't any left,' I said, quickly. 'With the King gone, they hadn't made many.'

'Then you should have come straight back,' said Scrope crossly.

'I couldn't,' I said. 'I was trying to coax Mrs Pennycod into making you one specially, and she'd just got her dough kneaded when she found that all the rabbit was used up.'

Mister Scrope grunted. I didn't think he believed me.

'Mrs Pennycod said she'd use some pigeon instead,' I went on before he could say anything, 'and if I go back just before sunset, she'll have it ready, nice and warm.'

'Then we mustn't disappoint her,' said Mister

Scrope, a greedy light in his eyes. 'Get on with your work now. You've a deal to do before then.'

I didn't say that he was the one going to be disappointed, waiting for the imaginary pie.

He looked up as a servant came in with a message. He read it and called Mark over to him. 'Master Cromwell needs a scribe at Lutterall House and you're to go straight to him, Mark,' he said. 'There's a cart waiting for you.'

'Yes, sir,' said Mark with a worried frown. 'Do I come back tonight – in the dark?'

'Don't be silly, boy,' said Mister Scrope. 'It's a three-hour journey. It would be too late to come back.'

Mark looked terrified as he packed up his quills and ink. 'I've never left London before,' he whispered in my ear.

'You'll be all right,' I whispered back. 'There aren't any dragons – at least not in Hertfordshire!'

Mark didn't laugh at the joke. He just looked paler.

'I wager Master Cromwell will be very pleased that it's you who has come,' I said, 'and not the new boy or the weasel.'

'Do you really think so?' he said, brightening a little. 'But what if I can't find my way round Lutterall House? I still get lost every time we move palaces with the King.'

'Why don't you draw a plan of the house?' I suggested. 'You know, how to get to the jakes from Cromwell's chamber and where to find your dinner and so on.'

'What a good idea,' said Mark with a huge grin.

He looked happier now. And I realised I was going to miss him while he was away.

26

Mister Scrope ushered me off to the kitchen well before six o'clock. Little did he know how long he might have to wait for his pigeon pie! I wouldn't be going anywhere near the kitchens. My target was Harrington. I planned to follow him and see where he went. As I hurried down the passage, a servant coming the other way gave me a friendly nod. How different from the day I'd arrived at the palace in my ragged clothes, I thought. I belonged here now, in my royal livery.

My livery! It was going to be dark soon but, if Harrington spotted me following him, I'd stick out a mile. And he might remember seeing me in his chamber. I went back to the scribes' room to get my rags.

Mister Scrope looked up hopefully.

'Just letting you know the pies are nearly ready,' I told him, secretly shoving my rags up my jerkin.

Down in the courtyard I passed a yeoman on horseback and I suddenly remembered that Cat would be waiting for me in the park for my riding lesson. If I went to tell her now, I might miss Harrington. I hoped she'd forgive me.

The last of the sun was lighting up the workshop roofs and casting long dark shadows across the flagstones. With no rich folk to please, only a few torches were lit, just enough to guide me towards the gate in the river wall.

When I got down onto the landing stage, I found there was almost nowhere to hide. Only an ornate barge tied to one of the mooring posts. I jumped on board, fought my way under the canvas cover and changed into my rags. I hoped the owner of the barge was at Lutterall House and wasn't going to row off with my livery once I'd gone.

I watched the steps from my canvas cover.

The bells chimed seven and then eight. As night fell the cold air began to creep into my thin clothes. I could barely feel my toes when I tried to wiggle them. If I didn't move soon, they'd drop off!

But that was nothing compared to the hunger that was gnawing at my belly.

The gate suddenly swung open and a figure limped down the steps. I recognised Hugh Harrington. He went to the end of the landing stage and hailed a passing boatman.

After a few moments a wherry appeared.

'What's the fare to Salt Wharf?' asked Harrington.

I didn't hear the answer, but Harrington shook his head and began to argue about the price. My mind raced. Harrington wasn't going to Chelsea, just as his servant had suspected. I'd heard of Salt Wharf. It was in the opposite direction. There was one big problem – how was I going to follow him if he took to the river? I realised I hadn't thought my plan through. I considered taking the barge, but I'd never be able to steer it in the right direction. And Harrington was likely to spot a huge, gold-leafed vessel bearing down on him.

He was holding out some coins now. The boatman took a lantern from his craft and held it up to inspect them. He'd agreed a fare. He'd be leaving any minute. And now I had an idea – a very risky one. The prow of the wherry was in darkness without the lantern and the men were turned away from me. Moving as slowly as a snail, I crept across the landing stage and climbed into the boat. I scrambled under the seat at the back. It was a tight squeeze. Suddenly the wherry rocked and Harrington came on board. He stumped over and sat down right above me.

'We're low in the water!' exclaimed the boatman as he strained on the oars to get the wherry back into the flow of the river.

The extra weight was me! Did he suspect he had more than one passenger? Harrington didn't say a thing.

'I warrant you're heavier than you look,' added the boatman.

'Mind your tongue!' snapped Harrington. 'I've paid for the passage, not your insults.'

I would have breathed a sigh of relief but I didn't have the space! The voyage seemed endless. I longed to stretch my legs. At last I felt the boat slow.

'Salt Wharf!' grunted the boatman and the boat hit something with a *clunk*. We'd docked.

Harrington got to his feet and the wherry gave a rolling lurch as he disembarked. If I wasn't quick, I'd lose him. But before I could follow, there came a cry.

'Hey there, boatman! Southwark if you please.'

The boat lurched again. More passengers were climbing aboard. I needed to disembark before I was taken off to the opposite bank of the river! I squirmed out from under the seat.

'Help!' screamed a plump woman who'd been about to plonk her bum on it. 'Murder!'

'You thieving little worm!' the wherryman shouted at me. 'Where's my fare?'

27

I didn't wait to explain. I shoved past them and leapt onto the wharf.

The wherryman lumbered after me, cursing. I saw Harrington ahead, halfway up a dark street. I had to shake off my pursuer.

I dived between some barrels. I heard the wherryman's heavy breathing as he searched for the swindling stowaway.

'Never mind him!' came a shout from the river. 'You'll lose our fare too if you don't take us immediately!'

The wherryman gave another curse and stamped off back to his boat.

Cautiously I peered out. I could just make out a distant figure, limping up the hill.

I followed, keeping close to the shadowy walls of the houses. The way was straight, though the houses leant in from either side to make a sort of tunnel and block out any moonlight. None of the buildings had seen a paintbrush or hammer and nails for a long time. I saw Harrington stop in a doorway. The door opened and he disappeared inside. I heard the sounds of bolts being drawn.

Harrington must have a secret purpose, or he wouldn't come in darkness to such a ramshackle place where footpads were sure to lurk. If it wasn't secret, he'd have told his servant where he was going. The only way to find out the truth was to get inside the house.

The downstairs window was too risky. Someone might be on the other side. The casement window on the floor above was shut, but the whole house leant at such an angle that there was a gap between the window and the frame.

The building next door had a wooden shop's canopy. I leapt to grab hold of it, swung my legs and pulled myself up. Balancing precariously, I reached over and began to push my fingers between the crooked frame and the window, trying to force it open.

I heard footsteps below and froze. A watchman was coming down the street, holding a lantern.

He stopped right beneath me. 'Nine of the clock and all's well!' he bellowed.

I made a hideous face, hoping that if he saw me he'd think I was a gargoyle, until I remembered that gargoyles usually hung on churches, not shops. He waved the light to and fro. I closed my eyes so the

146

light wouldn't reflect in them. I waited a long moment for him to challenge me but at last his footsteps faded into the distance. I tried the window again. It suddenly swung out towards me, with a loud creak, nearly knocking me off my perch.

I climbed quickly into the room, and listened to see if anyone had heard my entry. Men's voices rumbled from downstairs, but no footsteps approached. I groped silently about and came to a solitary table where I felt piles of papers. The breeze from the window sent them fluttering to the floor but I left it open as an escape route. I'd learnt my lesson.

My groping fingers found a candle stub and then a tinder box and char cloth. Soon I had some light to inspect the chamber. Apart from the table there was just a bare truckle bed in the corner. I began to sort through the scattered papers. Any small thing could be important. Each sheet was an unpaid bill run up by a John Westbury, courtier to the King. He'd accumulated large debts – owing for endless jewellery and fine clothes and a set of silver plates. Then I came across a vellum parchment with a broken seal.

'My good friend John,' I read. 'I await your arrival with great anticipation. Delgado the Spaniard will come to your home the night before our revelries, and you and Hugh will bring him to me. Delgado will know where he can best be accommodated once here. Be assured he is a most excellent archer and will provide fine entertainment for us on the feast of St

Benedict. He never fails to hit the bull's eye, although I will in any case ensure the prize bull is in full view at the moment of his triumph.'

The letter was signed Ralph Lutterall.

I read it again. On the surface, it seemed to be a friendly letter from Sir Ralph asking Westbury and Harrington to accompany an archer to his house. He mentioned the feast of St Benedict, which was tomorrow. Sir Ralph was arranging an impressive entertainment for his royal guest.

But why would they travel in the dangerous hours of darkness when they could easily go in daylight? Something else clanged discordantly in my head, like St Godric's bell after it was struck by lightning. I was just an abbey boy who'd been at Court a handful of days, but I didn't think they had bulls, prize or otherwise, at jousts.

The letter had an odd tone, telling but not telling, as if it was written in code. I knew Harrington to be a murderer and involved in something secret. Was Sir Ralph Lutterall also involved?

I slipped the letter inside my shirt, snuffed the candle and lifted the latch. I found myself on a small landing. The voices were clearer now. I looked down into the hall, which was lit by a small lamp. A flickering light showed under a door. I crept down the rickety stairs, my heart jumping with fear at every creak. Harrington was in the house somewhere. I dreaded that he'd find me, but I had to hear what was being said.

The door panelling was old, with slits and wormholes. I put my ear to the wood.

Two men were talking. I recognised Hugh Harrington's voice.

'. . . nothing I enjoy more than a display of . . . archery,' he was saying.

'And to have it when the joust is over and His Majesty is receiving the adulation of his loyal subjects.' I guessed this was John Westbury. 'The timing is immaculate. I drink to Ralph.'

Goblets clanged together in a toast.

'Did you really have to silence Talbot, though?' Westbury went on, lowering his voice. I pressed my ear harder to the door. 'We don't want any attention at this crucial time.'

Now I had another name to tell Cromwell – John Westbury was involved in this secret business. Once I had all the information I could glean, I'd find a way to get to Lutterall House and speak to my master.

'God's teeth, John!' exclaimed Harrington. A goblet slammed onto the table. 'If I hadn't killed him, who knows what else he'd have said? You weren't at Court. The pompous little windbag was telling the world how important he was about to become.'

'He was a loose cannon indeed,' said Westbury. 'Are you certain no one knows the truth about his death?'

'Everyone believes he died in a drunken brawl,' muttered Harrington. 'None of us is implicated. I even searched his stinking cesspit of a room afterwards and made sure nothing was left that might give us away.'

'Then you did well, Hugh,' Westbury said. 'Señor Delgado will be here soon and we'll be off. Take more wine while you wait. Ralph has planned every detail. Tomorrow our fortunes will be secure.'

'You'll be able to pay off all your debts, John,' said Harrington.

'Aye,' answered Westbury, 'and leave this wretched house at last.'

'Austin Friars will doubtless be available.' Harrington gave a cold laugh. 'I think it unlikely Master Cromwell will be living in it once we're in charge.'

This set my heart thumping. It sounded as if my master was in danger. Was a plot being hatched to remove him from his position close to the King?

'Where is the Spaniard?' exclaimed Harrington. I heard footsteps pacing the room. 'This waiting is too much!'

'Calm yourself, Hugh,' said Westbury soothingly. 'Drink your wine, and try this beef. And think of the fare we shall eat once this is over.'

'I've no stomach for food while the threat of the executioner spilling our guts hangs over us,' replied Harrington.

The executioner! Being hanged, drawn and quartered was a punishment reserved for high treason. To my horror, I realised that these men must be conspiring, not against Cromwell, but against the King himself!

'Don't think of the hangman, Hugh,' began Westbury.

'Think of the future. It will be others who swing. Our young lady . . .'

'. . . who will be a puppet in our hands,' interjected Harrington.

'Indeed,' agreed John Westbury. 'Our young puppet will be doing everything *we* say, little knowing who brought about her great good fortune.'

'To our Princess – soon to be *Queen* Mary.'

I could hardly breathe as his words struck home. Now at last I understood Talbot's letter. Drink had overtaken him as he'd been about to write *Princess Mary*. Princess Mary—the King's daughter and heir to the throne of England. Harrington and Westbury were talking as if she was soon going to be Queen. Yet I knew she could not ascend the throne unless her father was dead.

The plot was indeed high treason. These men intended to kill King Henry.

I thought about what Sir Ralph had written. An archer, the Spaniard, would hit the bull's eye and the prize bull would be in full view. It was no ordinary sport he was describing in his letter. I felt my blood turn to ice. The prize bull was none other than King Henry himself.

The horrific scene unfolded in my head. The King would take part in an archery competition against Delgado. I knew His Majesty could never resist testing his skill against other expert marksmen. He'd have no idea that this would be his final contest. The treacherous Spaniard would pull back his bowstring and, while the crowd watched with anticipation, swing round and loose his deadly arrow at the King.

I had enough evidence to lay before Master Cromwell. I had to get to Lutterall House before the traitors.

I turned towards the stairs, but my sleeve caught on a splinter of wood, making the door shudder in its frame. I froze, hoping no one had noticed, but my luck was out. Something crashed against the door. I staggered back in shock as I heard an angry bark.

'What's the matter with that dog?' said Harrington irritably. 'Is there someone out there?'

'Rats, most likely,' Westbury replied. 'This wretched house is running with them. Shut your noise, Sabre!' Sabre barked again. I heard a curse and the click of a latch.

The door was flung open and a massive dog burst out, its teeth bared in a snarl. With one leap, it had me pinned helplessly under its huge paws.

28

'Sabre's caught a rat,' came Harrington's mocking voice.

'Good boy!' said his companion. I couldn't see his face. My vision was full of slavering jaws. 'Now leave the vermin!' The dog refused to move. Then suddenly it was dragged away by its collar. It pulled and snarled, desperate to get at its prey.

'Who's this?' snapped Harrington, bringing a candle over while John Westbury fought to keep the dog off me. 'You said you'd sent your servant away, John.'

Harrington had seen me yesterday. Only once – but he might recognise me as a palace servant, even without my livery. It was time for Simkins to make an appearance. As Harrington seized the front of my jerkin and wrenched me to my feet, I contorted my face, hunched my shoulders to my ears and began to whimper.

'I've never seen him before in my life,' called Westbury.

'I meant no harm,' I pleaded, pitching my voice high. 'Don't hurt poor Simkins. I only wanted a coin or two. Me mum and me five brothers are starving and we've nothing to buy bread.' I squinted up at Harrington. 'Just a coin, mister?'

'A coin!' spat Harrington. 'I'll warrant you were skulking out there, listening to our talk. We don't reward spies.'

I gave a whine of fear. That came easily enough. Harrington may not have remembered me but it was small comfort. These men were prepared to kill the King. I wouldn't be getting any mercy.

'He's just a common thief,' said Westbury, still struggling with the dog, who seemed desperate to bury its teeth in me.

'Thief or spy, what are we going to do with him?' demanded Harrington.

Westbury gave a nasty laugh. 'Kill him, of course!'

'I heard nothing, I swear it,' I said desperately.

Harrington threw me into a corner of the room. I slammed against a writing table. Everything on it crashed to the floor. I pushed myself painfully into an awkward sitting position.

'Fetch a rope,' snapped Harrington.

A rope? Were they going to hang me? I'd been plunged into a nightmare but there was to be no happy waking. I writhed and kicked until Harrington clouted mc, making my head reel with dizziness.

Westbury was soon back with the rope. I cringed back in a feeble attempt to stop Harrington looping it round my neck. But that wasn't what he was after. Instead, he yanked my hands together and began to tie them. In my relief I almost forgot to keep my Simkins face.

'We won't kill you here,' he told me. 'We don't want to leave a rotting corpse cluttering up the place.'

My death had been postponed for the moment. My head was still swimming from the blow, but I had to make a plan. As my hands were bound, I pushed them against the force of the rope to create a space. It was too small for Harrington to notice – barely enough room for an acorn. As my captor turned his attention to my ankles, I checked my ploy had worked. The rope was slightly loose.

'We don't want him yelling,' said Westbury, snatching a napkin from the table. He forced it between my teeth and tied it so tightly that the cloth cut into my cheeks. 'Sabre, guard!' The dog bounded over, slavering, sizing me up for his dinner, no doubt.

There was a faint knock on the front door. Both men wheeled round. My heart leapt. If I could make myself heard I might be rescued. Westbury went to answer the knock.

'Señor Delgado has arrived,' he announced as he returned.

My hope of rescue deflated like a burst pig's bladder.

A man with a pointed beard came in behind Westbury. He carried a longbow on his back and ducked to avoid it catching the door lintel. He looked nervously round, giving a start when he saw me bound and gagged.

'Who is this?' he said in a heavily accented voice.

'A petty thief,' replied Westbury shortly. 'We'll be disposing of him when we go.'

Harrington passed the Spanish archer a goblet and pushed the platter of meat across the table towards him. 'You have your instructions?'

The Spaniard nodded.

John Westbury poured himself some wine and raised his glass. 'And now a toast. Gentlemen – to our future Queen. Long may she reign.'

'Long may she reign under our . . . expert guidance,' laughed Harrington.

'Aye to that,' agreed Westbury. 'Directly the deed is done you will have the pleasure of riding to break the sad news to the poor Princess.'

'But what of me?' broke in Delgado. There was an anxious edge to his voice. 'You will make sure I am not caught?'

'My friend, you have nothing to fear,' Westbury assured him. 'In the chaos you will be smuggled out of the country – with a purse full of gold for a job well done.'

As they spoke I cast my eyes around me. Scattered over the floor were the ink, the paper, the quills and even the knife to trim them. *What a grim joke, to be surrounded by the tools of my trade in my final hours*, I thought to myself. Pen and ink were no use to me now, but the knife might be – if I could only get hold of it. I slowly moved my bound hands towards it. At once Sabre let out a low warning growl. I stopped still.

Westbury tossed down a bone. Sabre fell on it. I risked moving my hand. The dog ignored the movement. Slowly I leant forwards and tried to grasp the handle of the knife with my fingertips. The knife spun round, making a sound on the wooden floorboards that sounded like thunder to me, but the men were too busy eating and discussing their bright future to hear, and Sabre was chomping noisily at his bone. I stretched a little further. This time I caught the handle between my forefingers. I pulled it gradually towards me.

Sabre suddenly raised his head. I froze. He glared at me for a moment, saliva dripping from his mouth, then went back to his chewing. I eased the knife into the gap between my hands and slowly lifted them, as if I was praying to the heavens for help. The knife slid into my sleeve. I felt the cold bronze handle reach my elbow.

The men thumped their tankards on the table and Westbury left the room. He was soon back, carrying a sack. I was just wondering what it was for when he threw it over my head.

I tried to struggle free but the men were too strong for me. I was encased in the rough sacking, lifted into the air and swung and jolted in equal measure.

'Lock the door behind us, Delgado,' came Westbury's voice. 'We don't want any more thieves creeping in.'

I heard their boots on the cobbles. We were in the street then. And I was being taken to my death. I pulled at the bonds around my wrists. They didn't give. I tried to slip one hand out. The rope burned my skin and it was almost impossible as I was tossed about. The two men carrying me spoke together in low voices.

'It was a stroke of genius to use a Spaniard for the killing,' Westbury was saying. 'Nobody knows our connection with the man.'

'When he's caught,' added Harrington, 'which we will make sure of, it will not matter how much information is squeezed out of him at the Tower.'

I realised that Delgado was not within earshot.

'You speak truly,' said Westbury, 'for who will believe a Spaniard? We all know that Spain is angry with Henry for rejecting Queen Katherine. Everyone will think he was an agent of the Emperor sent to get revenge.'

An idea began to form in my mind. If the Spaniard was to find out what was being planned for him, surely he wouldn't go through with the killing. If I could just get the gag off my mouth, I could shout a warning. I might risk a knife in my ribs from the conspirators, but the King's life was more important.

Ignoring the searing pain I tried again to pull my hands from the bonds.

I heard Harrington's voice. 'Here's the place!'

The men stopped. I felt the sack begin to swing and then I was suddenly flying through the air, tumbling over and over. I started to plummet. Instinctively I curled up, bracing myself for the landing.

There was a jolt and a rush of freezing water and now I knew my fate. I'd been thrown into the River Thames. I was going to drown.

29

I was sinking in the deadly cold of the river.

The water rushed through the sacking, stinging my skin like icy fingers. I tried to clamp my lips shut over the gag to stop the filthy taste of the Thames from seeping into my mouth. I yanked desperately at my bonds and kicked my bound legs for the surface, pushing against the sack and the river that sucked me down to its bed. I'd need air soon. I strained again at my ropes and felt my skin tearing. I'd made sure my hands weren't tied tightly, so why couldn't I release them?

Brother Matthew's voice suddenly came into my head. 'You're being too hasty as usual, Jack.'

Fighting all my instincts, I made myself slow down. I twisted my wrists in my bonds. One hand came free! The sack was clinging to me like a skin but I managed to push it away and rip the gag off.

I pulled the knife from my sleeve and hacked through the rope holding my feet, ignoring the pain as I cut into my ankle. Now I slashed at the sack. But I was flailing blindly in the pitch-black water of the flowing river and my lungs were screaming for air. The sack seemed to taunt me, gripping tightly to my arms. I slashed again and again. Finally I felt the knife rip through the rough sacking. I dropped the knife and tore it open with my fingers, forcing myself through.

I kicked hard, giving silent thanks for the times at the abbey when I'd sneaked down to the pond and taught myself to swim. But I'd never been in a deep, pounding river before. I felt it pulling me down. With a last effort I thrashed upwards. Then, just when I thought my lungs would burst, my head broke the surface. I was alive.

A wave splashed my face, almost choking me as I gulped in the wonderful cold air. I wondered if my frozen limbs would have the strength to take me to the jetty I could see on the bank. I didn't care which bank it was. It was close. That was enough. But the current grew stronger as I swam towards it and rough water swirled round the wooden struts. I tried to stop myself being taken along but my strength was no match for the river. I was sucked under the jetty. Something hit me in the chest and the breath was knocked from my lungs.

I found myself hanging over a log, wedged between two struts. I lay there like a limp rag for a minute, gathering my strength. Then I hauled my body against the force of the water towards one of the struts and clung on, begging my tired muscles not to give up now.

Teeth chattering, I inched my way up onto the jetty, trying to find footholds on the slippery wood. At last I collapsed onto the cold, slimy boards. My body was telling me to curl up and sleep, but I forced my frozen brain to stay awake.

In a few short hours, the King would be taking part in the archery contest at Lutterall House. He little suspected he would be going to his death. The one person who could warn him of his mortal danger was me. And I'd never be able to walk there in time – even if I knew which way to go. I would have to ask Cat for help.

I dragged myself to my feet. I felt the blood from the cut on my ankle running down my foot and my wrists throbbed from the rope weals, but they were of no matter. In the moonlight I saw that I was on the north bank. Follow that and I'd come to Whitehall – eventually.

✿

My journey seemed endless. I had no idea of time and as I stumbled along I feared the sun would rise and I'd still be miles from the palace. The conspirators would be well on their way to Lutterall House by now.

The wind got up, cutting through my wet rags. The cold bit into me and my whole body was wracked with shivering. I tried to run to warm up but I had no strength for anything more than a faltering walk. Even at that pace, I panted as I moved. I stopped and leant my back against the river wall, alarmed as I felt drowsiness drift over me. The yearning to sleep was overwhelming. My head fell to my chest, but the jerking movement was enough to wake me. Strangely, I stopped shivering and my breathing slowed. It made my head swim. Was I no longer cold? It didn't make sense – but nothing did, except the one certainty that I must get to Cat. That one thought drove me on. I remember very little more, but I must have forced myself along the rest of the journey, half alive and half dead, until I finally came in sight of the Whitehall stairs where Harrington had taken the wherry. I'd made it to the palace.

Everywhere was quiet as I dragged myself through the dark passages, past sleeping servants, towards the sewing room. My feet were numb from cold and I was dully surprised they were still working. At last I came upon Cat, curled up beside others in a corner. I nudged her with my foot. She muttered something about winding bobbins and kept sleeping. I tried again. Her eyes flew open.

'You're a bit late for your riding,' she hissed, sitting bolt upright. 'I waited for nearly an hour last night. You can't expect me to—'

I raised a wobbly finger to my lips. 'Help!' I croaked, through chattering teeth.

For a moment her eyes stared wildly at me in the

dark. Then she scrambled to her feet and beckoned to me to follow. I staggered and clutched her to stop myself falling.

She quickly slipped my arm over her shoulder.

She helped me into an empty workshop where she lit a fire, gasping as the flames showed up my wounds and soaking clothes. She bustled about the room, found a warm cloak and wrapped it round me. 'You won't mind it needs repair,' she said. 'Now, where's your livery?'

I described the barge where I'd stowed it.

Cat raised her eyebrows. 'I hope it's still there,' she said as she disappeared.

I sat in an exhausted stupor. My brain felt like a pool of mud, too thick for any thoughts to stir. And yet something was trying to pull its way out. I focused on it, wondering what my mind was trying to tell me. And then all at once it came sharply into my head. The letter.

The letter! I'd been too exhausted to think about it. Did I still have the vital evidence? Fingers numb with cold, I fumbled inside my shirt. Yes, there it was. I pulled it out, careful not to tear the sopping paper. I held my breath as I peeled open the folds, dreading that it might disintegrate in my hands.

It was intact, every damning word plain to see. Not even the mighty Thames could make the ink run. That warmed me more than any fire. I laid out the letter to dry it.

Cat bustled in with my livery in her hands. While I changed she scuttled off again for strips of cloth and a big chunk of bread. I hadn't realised how hungry I was. I wolfed it down.

'Now you can tell me what happened to you,' she said, as she bound my wounds.

'I followed Hugh Harrington,' I said, between bites, 'and I found out what he's up to. He's plotting to murder the King! There'll be an archery contest and King Henry will be killed.'

Cat's hands flew to her mouth.

'He'll be at Lutterall House already – with John Westbury and a Spaniard called Delgado. They're in league with Sir Ralph Lutterall.'

'The names don't matter!' said Cat impatiently. 'We've got to stop them!'

I reached out and took her hand. 'It's very important that you remember the names,' I told her.

'Why?'

'Because you're the only other person who knows of this plot,' I explained. 'If anything happens to me . . .'

'Don't even say it!' she whispered. 'Anyway, you'll be safe here. We'll . . . send a messenger to warn the King.'

'We can't tell a messenger,' I said. 'We don't know who else to trust. No, I have to go to Lutterall House myself – before it's too late.'

'But who can you trust there?' asked Cat.

'There is one man,' I said slowly. I had been told to tell no one of my special work for Cromwell, but I had to tell Cat. If I didn't make it to Lutterall House, she could tell my master about the plot. And I felt I owed her the truth.

'I didn't just happen upon this mystery,' I said. 'Master Cromwell set me a secret task. I was to listen to Talbot for words of treachery.'

She looked at me for a long moment. 'Are you a spy?' she whispered.

'Not really,' I said. 'I was never meant to do more than overhear his conversation. The rest I did of my own accord.'

Cat almost looked impressed.

'And he'll take your word about this plot?' she asked.

'I think so,' I said. 'I've got proof.'

I showed her the drying letter.

'What does it say?' demanded Cat, frowning at the words that must have looked like scribbled nonsense to her.

She nodded slowly as I read it to her. 'I'll take you to Lutterall House,' she said at last. 'We'll ride Diablo!'

I shook my head. 'I'm not getting you into danger. Get a horse ready for me and I'll go.'

'After one riding lesson?' asked Cat incredulously. 'And in the state you're in? That would be madness. I won't have anything to do with it.'

'I'm warm now,' I said, trying to believe it myself. I got to my feet and staggered towards the door. I could hear the sounds of servants beginning to wake up. 'I haven't time to argue. I'll do it myself.'

'A fine idea,' said Cat, 'with only two drawbacks. One, you wouldn't know which horse to take, and two, you'd never get it tacked up. Oh, I quite forgot. There's a third. You can't ride!'

I threw off the cloak and flung my arms out in despair. 'Then the King will die.'

30

Ten minutes later I was standing in a stable staring at a grey horse with its nose in a bucket of oats. The letter was safe inside my shirt again.

The feeling had come back into my feet now and it was all I could do not to shout at the fierce pins and needles.

Cat hurried in, carrying a saddle and bridle. 'I don't know why I've agreed to this,' she muttered. She slung the saddle over the horse's back and pulled the girth tight. 'You're lucky Mumble's owner has gone to her family in Wales. Mumble should be quiet and easy – though I think you're mazed to try.'

'I hope you won't get into trouble,' I said.

'Me?' said Cat, easing the bit into Mumble's soft mouth. 'You're the one who'll get into trouble. I shall take a farthing's wager on it. Will it be ditch, hedge or pond? My money's on the ditch.'

I frowned, puzzled.

'I'm just wondering where you'll fall,' Cat told me airily. She led Mumble outside to a quiet place at the back of the stables, next to a steaming dung heap.

'Well, you'll lose your money,' I said. 'I won't be falling off.'

Cat heaved me onto the horse's back so hard I nearly fell off into the dung. I was privately relieved to find that the ground wasn't nearly as far away as on Diablo. I took up the reins.

'This is serious, Cat! It's my only chance of stopping something terrible.' I hesitated. 'Look, if anything . . . happens to me, would you also get a message to Brother Matthew at St Godric's Abbey? He's my godfather.'

'Nothing's going to happen to you,' said Cat fiercely. 'I hope,' she added.

I'd been all right until I heard those last two words. Now I had a sudden urge to leap off Mumble's back and hide in the dung heap and forget my mission.

Cat stroked the horse's neck. 'Have you got the letter?'

'Of course.' I patted my jerkin.

It was probably my exhaustion but, suddenly, in my head, I was back outside the abbey, with Brother Matthew checking that I had the letter for Master Thynne. A grim thought came to me – everything that had happened to me in the past few days hinged on the written word. The simple act of putting quill to paper could change a life – or end it.

I was brought back to the present by Cat.

'Then go – and good luck,' she was saying. 'And I must go too and make it appear I've been in my sleeping corner all night or questions will be asked.'

She ran off.

'Gee up, Mumble!' I muttered nervously, squeezing my legs to make her move.

The mare ignored me. I clicked my tongue as I'd heard Cat do, but the horse was only interested in having some breakfast from a nearby bush.

I began to wonder if I'd have been better off on Diablo! At least I'd get there quickly – if by some miracle I managed to hold on. In desperation I broke off a long twig from a nearby tree. Mumble's ears pricked as she heard the crack of the wood. I didn't want to hit her so I waved the stick feebly over her head. The sight of a whip turned Mumble into Diablo! She gave a loud whinny, tossed her head and charged off towards King Street. I clung to the saddle for dear life, fearing that if this was Mumble's first ride for a while she'd have the energy of three horses.

A few servants and workmen were already about, though it wasn't sunrise yet. They scattered at the sight of the charging horse. As we careered past the Charing Cross, I managed to get enough control of the reins to get Mumble to turn left and take the north road. Cat had told me this was the way to go and had barely concealed her pleasure that the route was something else she knew and I didn't. But I didn't care about that.

'Get to Lutterall House' repeated in my head like a drumbeat.

'Don't forget,' Cat had insisted, 'the north road will take you to St Martin's field and then keep to that road until you see the George Inn.'

I bumped along, clinging to the saddle. However, it turned out my trusty steed didn't want to gallop all the way after all. She walked or trotted instead – with the occasional burst of speed and sudden stops for breakfast from tasty hedgerows.

Cat had said it should take about an hour to get to the inn. But by the time I saw a battered saint and dragon on a battered board swinging outside a battered inn, I would have sworn that the whole morning had passed.

At the George Inn the road forked. Cat had assured me I was to head left and, after another hour or so, I'd see a milestone saying London and here I'd find the lane to Lutterall House. She had made it sound simple and I had to trust she was right.

I could see that the road to the left was deeply rutted, as if many a cart had passed by recently. I told myself that, even without Cat's directions, I'd have seen this clue and followed it. Courtiers on horseback and cartloads of provisions had gone that way to Lutterall House for the King's visit. They'd left me a trail.

My bum – the only bit of me that wasn't already aching from my night ordeal – was sore with jolting by the time I realised that we'd gone wrong. I'd been concentrating so hard on staying in the saddle that I hadn't been looking out for the milestone. Now I realised that the road ahead was no longer churned up with hundreds of cart and horse tracks. The royal party couldn't have come this way yesterday. I pulled hard on the reins and for a change Mumble obeyed. She gradually came to a halt outside a cottage where a man was up early, mending a thatched roof. I was about to congratulate myself on my expert horsemanship when I realised she'd only stopped because she'd spotted some tasty grass.

'Hey there, good fellow,' I called to the man. 'Is this the road for Lutterall House?'

The man scratched his head. 'Aye, if you're wanting to go right around the world to reach it,' he said with a wry grin. 'It's back the way you've come. There's a milestone for London by the road. You want to turn west there. That'll bring you to the big house.'

I stifled my curses, thanked the man and pulled on a rein to make Mumble turn. At first she ignored me, but finally made a clumsy figure of eight and ambled the wrong way up the road. In desperation I slapped her on the rump. The next second I found myself charging back past the cottage.

The worker wished me 'God's speed' and I heard him chuckling.

When I reached the milestone I had the devil's own job to get Mumble to turn down the little lane, but now I knew I was back on the right road. It was covered in horse and wheel tracks. I was nearly at my destination and I reckoned my horse was finally under my control.

I was wrong. The sudden squawk of a magpie startled Mumble into a gallop. We came to a sharp bend – and I could tell that she wasn't going to take it.

Instead she was charging straight for a high hedge. Was this horse missing her hunting days?

There was only one thing for an expert horseman to do – I shut my eyes. The next instant I was catapulted out of the saddle. I felt myself flying through the air for the second time that day, but this time the landing was harder and the breath was knocked out of my body. I opened my eyes. I was lying in a heap in a ploughed field, listening to Mumble's hoofbeats fading into the distance. Dazed, I stumbled to my feet, muttering oaths at the horse as I clambered over the furrows back to the road. *At least Cat has lost her bet,* I thought grimly. *She didn't mention a field.*

I hobbled as fast as I could down the lane.

The sun was shining low through the trees behind me. It was still early. I couldn't believe it had only taken me a few hours to get here. However, I'd heard that King Henry was quick to rise on fine mornings like this so I couldn't waste time.

The red brick and tall chimneys of Lutterall House came into view through the trees. Behind the house I glimpsed the wooden tiltyard, decorated with rows of pennants to impress the King. I listened. There was no sign that the entertainment had started, no sounds of horses' hooves or crowds cheering.

I was in time. Now to find Master Cromwell.

Then something made me stop in my tracks. A whole crowd of Sir Ralph's servants, in their silver and green livery, was running across the courtyard to the house. Their talk was hurried and breathless. The whole place was buzzing with some dreadful news.

My heart in my mouth, I raced up to a man carrying a pail of water.

'What's happened?' I blurted out.

The man looked at me in amazement. 'Where have you been that you do not know?' he said. 'Rolling about in some field instead of working, by the looks of you.'

'I . . . had an accident,' I said lamely. 'But tell me what's going on.'

'It's His Majesty,' said the man. 'He's been struck down!'

31

My head spun. I'd come too late. If only I'd been a better rider. If only I'd arrived sooner. If only . . .

But the man was still talking. 'He has such a headache as he's never known. You could hear him bellow from here to kingdom come.'

'A headache?' I was stunned. 'Just a headache?'

The man lowered his voice. 'A *royal* headache, if you please! Well, if you want to know what I think, our noble monarch would have done better with less shouting. Bound to make it worse! But don't say I said so. Be that as it may, his physician gave him a drink of lavender and sage and whatnot and now he's a bit better. And that's lucky for us, I'll warrant, for we all remember the other remedy. How would they have got the noose from a hanged man to press on the royal forehead, I should like to know!'

'So he won't be taking part in the sport today,' I said, relief flooding through me.

'Oh, yes, he will!' said the man. 'His Majesty, God bless him, is already drinking wine in his tent in the tiltyard, ready to appear when everyone's assembled. And he doesn't like to be kept waiting. That's why we're all rushing about to get his noble audience ready. The King will watch others joust, as he always does, so I hear, before capping them with his greater skill. I'd love to watch, but that's not to be.'

'Isaac!' came a shout from one of the outbuildings. 'Where's that water?'

'Coming!' Isaac picked up his pail and rushed off.

I ran towards the tiltyard, trying to brush the mud from my livery. If the King was already there, then Master Cromwell would surely be with him. Dodging a line of men weighed down with meat and wine flagons, I could see the whole of the jousting arena. Sir Ralph Lutterall had put on a fine show for his monarch. No one would suspect that he had deadly plans. Bright wooden walls, painted silver and green, had been built round three sides with large open gates on the fourth. Inside, a long, low fence ran the length of the track, just like the one at Whitehall. Two towers were set at either end. The King's royal red and blue flags flew from the top, their gold lions and feathers glinting as the sun touched them. Armoured horses were tied up next to striped tents. The riders would be inside, having their own armour strapped on. One tent was larger than all the others – a magnificent thing with the royal standard flying from its pointed roof. That was where I had to go.

Yeomen guards surrounded the outside of the tiltyard and, further away in the grounds, King Henry's Gentlemen of the Spears patrolled on their richly clad horses. I'd only heard of them before. The riders and their steeds were magnificent. I looked for the archery targets that would have been set up somewhere in the parklands. From where I stood I couldn't see them, but I was sure they were there, ready for the fatal sport that Lutterall and his cronies had planned.

Courtiers were hurrying to the tiltyard to be there before the King made his stately entrance. The villains were somewhere at Lutterall House and I knew I mustn't be spotted. I didn't think they'd recognise me as the ragamuffin they'd tossed in the Thames now that I was in my livery, but I couldn't take that chance.

I crept along behind a band of servants carrying seat cushions. I felt every bruise and cut from my long night but I wasn't going to let that stop me. In the middle of the long wall inside the tiltyard was a tiered stand. That must be for the King and the most favoured of his Court. Every seat was taken by grandly dressed men and women. I suddenly saw Westbury among the crowd and quickly averted my face.

A platform had been constructed in front of the stand. For the victors to receive their accolades, I supposed. My view was blocked for a moment by latecomers hurrying in. I focused my attention on the centre of the royal stand. It was covered in a tapestry and hung with banners. Three chairs had been placed under a satin canopy. The huge central chair – carved and painted in gold – stood empty.

The King's place, I thought. Lady Anne Boleyn sat to its right, leaning across and talking to a white-haired man seated on the other side. I'd bet the stars this was Sir Ralph Lutterall himself. He wore a hat, like many of the other men, but this one was of bright blue velvet – and it sported a long peacock feather. He was listening, smiling and inclining his head at her words, playing the gracious host. A cold shudder ran up my back at the sight of his calm deception.

And now I spotted Cromwell. He was sitting behind Lady Anne, deep in conversation with someone. I rushed forwards to the gates.

Two halberds came clanging down in front of me, barring my way.

'Where do you think you're going, Jack Briars?'

It was Nicholas Mountford. He smiled and began to lower his weapon, but the other man kept his stoutly in my path.

'I must speak with Master Cromwell,' I said. 'Please let me through.'

'I'm surprised you bother to ask,' joked Mountford. 'After clambering all over Whitehall, surely you could scale these walls with no trouble.' He glanced at my uniform. 'It looks as if you've been up to some such mischief already.'

'I'd rather walk this time, if it's all right with you,' I tried to joke back.

The other yeoman smiled too. 'This must be the acrobatic boy you told us about, Nicholas. Well, Jack Briars, I'm sorry we can't let you in, for you'd probably add to the fun!'

'It'll just have to wait, Jack,' Nicholas Mountford told me. 'We have our orders. None but the guests are to watch the entertainment.'

'But you must let me pass,' I insisted. 'It is of vital importance.'

'You're aiming to see the joust, more like,' said Mountford's companion. 'Take my advice, lad, and don't stay around here. We don't want His Majesty falling over a loitering servant when he comes out after the contest.'

I was helpless. I couldn't tell these men my business. I had no idea who was involved in the conspiracy. There was no other way to get to my master. Even the greatest acrobat in the world wouldn't get over those walls without a spear in his back. I heard the gates swing shut and caught the sound of trumpets from the tiltyard. A great roar went up. His Majesty must have appeared.

I felt defeated, but then I realised there might be one more chance to stop Delgado and his lethal arrow. The archery was to be straight after the joust. It would take place somewhere in the grounds. I'd catch Master Cromwell as he made his way there. Delgado was to show his skill before he made the fatal shot – or so the letter had said. I glanced back towards the gates. Nicholas Mountford stood alone there now.

'You mustn't hang around here, Jack,' he told me. 'You heard what Samuel Compton said.'

'I know,' I said, putting on a sad face, 'and he was right. I just wanted to see the joust. But as I can't, I thought I'd hide somewhere and watch the archery instead. Do you know where it will be?'

'You don't give up, do you?' laughed Mountford. 'Sorry to disappoint you, but there's no archery planned for today, only the joust.'

'There must be!' I gasped. 'I overheard . . . someone talking about it.'

'Then you overheard wrong,' said Nicholas Mountford. 'Seems you won't be seeing any entertainment. Best get back to your work before you're missed, Jack.'

I nodded dumbly and walked away. None of this made sense. There had to be archery. That was where Delgado was going to kill the King. In desperation I looked again at the letter.

The words hit me like the deadliest archer's arrow. *I will ensure the prize bull is in full view at the moment of his triumph.* My heart began to thud in my chest. I had misunderstood. The triumph that Sir Ralph Lutterall had written about wasn't Delgado's at the archery – it was the King's at the joust. The prize bull – King Henry – would be in full view *on the platform*. He would take off his helmet and receive the adoration of the crowd. That was when Delgado would make his fatal shot.

And the joust was about to begin.

32

My brain felt as if it was wrapped in swaddling blankets from lack of sleep. I shook myself.

'Where would Delgado be?' I muttered. He wouldn't be among the spectators, that was certain. He'd look too suspicious with a huge longbow on his back, so he'd have to shoot from outside the tiltyard. I stared stupidly at the wooden walls. To my tired mind they swayed against the sky. I tried to think what I'd do if I was the marksman. I'd be searching for somewhere high so that my shot cleared those walls.

The house itself was the only place tall enough – and near enough to his target. I hoped to spot Delgado lurking on the roof, but of course he wasn't. Then something moved in a window just below the eaves. I fixed my gaze on it, wondering if it was just the reflection of a bird or a cloud. But there it was again! That was no bird. Someone was up there.

I noted the position of the window and sped towards the house, darting between the surprised servants, who were still busy about their tasks. I took the nearest entrance and found myself in the kitchen. Red-faced cooks and their minions, sweat pouring down their faces, ran around like piglets in a sty.

I skirted round them, making for some steps at the other end. They led up to a hall. No one would mind if I took the main stairs, I decided. I'd barely taken a pace when someone came out of a room. A tall man with a limp. It was Hugh Harrington. I shrank back before he saw me.

I slipped away into the kitchen and spotted a platter of pies cooling on the side. I swept it up and returned to the hall, the smell taunting my empty stomach.

'Make way,' I cried, holding the platter on my shoulder to hide my face. 'Pies for the King. He wants them in his bedchamber – for later,' I added quickly.

A servant coming towards the kitchen fell back as he heard the important destination of the pasties. Forcing myself not to run, I marched to the main staircase and began to climb.

'Hey!' I froze. That was Harrington's voice. 'You there!'

I turned as if responding to a command and nearly dropped the platter in relief. Harrington wasn't talking to me. He was demanding something from a boy in Lutterall livery.

I vanished up the stairs.

Long passages ran off from either side. I had no idea where the next staircase was.

'Jack!' Mark Helston was coming along the passage, a broad grin on his face. 'So they wanted your help too! I'm so pleased to see you.' I wished I could have said the same, but the minutes were flying by. Mark flapped a piece of paper at me. 'Your idea of a map has been so useful.' He opened it out. 'I've made floor plans and I haven't got lost once despite this being a labyrinth of a house. See, we're here.' He prodded the paper with his finger. 'There's the main staircase. And those lines are another one. And here's Cromwell's chamber, on the top floor, which is where I'm off to now to fetch some letters.'

If Cromwell's chamber was on the top floor, then the chamber I was searching for must be nearby. I slammed the pies down on a nearby chest – well, all but one, which I gobbled up, to Mark's horror.

'Take me there now!' I told him, my mouth full.

'What?' Mark looked at me as if I'd gone mad. 'Master Cromwell's at the sport.' He suddenly noticed my clothes. 'And I advise you to smarten up before you present yourself to him.'

'It's not him I want,' I said. 'I need to get to the top of the house and you know the quickest way. It's very important.'

Mark didn't move.

'Run!' I urged, pulling at his sleeve.

Mark nodded dumbly, looked at his map and set off.

I ran after him. He paused at every turn, checking the way. I'd never have found the stairs without him.

Mark stopped at the top of the stairs, panting. He pointed down the passageway to first door on the left. 'That's . . .' he began.

'Shhh!' I warned, putting my finger to my lips.

Mark's eyes darted around in terror.

'That's Cromwell's chamber,' he mouthed. It was on the opposite side of the house to the joust, so the room I was after must be on the other side of the passage. I needed the one at the end. That was where Delgado could be lurking.

'Thank you, Mark,' I whispered. 'Now go. I can't tell you what's going on. It might put you in danger. But it's very important.'

'What about you?' Mark whispered back. 'If it's dangerous, you shouldn't stay either.'

'I've got no choice,' I muttered grimly, pushing him towards Cromwell's room. 'Forget you saw me.'

He tiptoed into the chamber.

And then there was silence. No one else seemed to be about.

But then an assassin wouldn't be announcing his presence, I thought. I crept to the door at the end. I hoped that Delgado would be intent on his work. If I was quiet I'd get across the room before he knew I was there, and leap on him or bring him to the ground or, better still, push him out of the window. Unfortunately that would make me a murderer, but I felt sure the

King would pardon me when I told him my story.

I tensed as I lifted the latch and pushed on the door. The room was empty! The window was open and the bed curtain had been caught by the wind and was draped over the window frame. It flapped in the breeze, looking for all the world as if it was waving at the people below.

This was my killer, I thought bitterly, pulling the curtain free. But I'd got one thing right. There was a fine view of the joust from this window.

Two men in armour were galloping towards each other along the tiltyard below. The drum of the hoofbeats reached me, then the gasp of the crowd as the lances clashed. I glanced towards the royal seats. Even at this distance, I could see the King was not there. I searched feverishly for the huge figure. There he was in his bright silver armour, standing by his horse at the end of the track. He would be jousting next!

So surely the assassin must be in one of these chambers, waiting his moment. I'd have to check them all. The King hadn't mounted his horse yet. I prayed I had time.

Suddenly a harsh cawing came from somewhere in the grounds. I looked towards the sound – a herb garden stretched out below me, and beyond it stood a thick copse of trees.

A spiky pine, taller than the others, rose in the middle of the spinney. Crows were flying around it, screeching angrily. They'd been disturbed. That was all it was. My nerves were getting the better of me.

But as I turned from the window, something caught my eye. For the briefest of seconds an arm flashed out at the angry birds. Now I knew what had disturbed them. There was a man in the tree.

33

I was certain it was Delgado. It was the perfect place for an assassin to hide. I was amazed he could fire an arrow from that far with accuracy, but he must know his craft.

Sending silent thanks to Mark and his map, I made it down to the ground floor like a terrier down a rabbit hole. The crows were still circling and screeching when I stepped outside. The trumpeters struck up again. The sharp sound cut through the air. They were announcing that it was the King's turn to joust. The crowd roared. Time was running out.

Empty baskets were stacked by a log pile just outside the kitchen door. I slung one onto my shoulder and set off through the herb garden. If Delgado was keeping watch, I hoped he'd ignore a wood-gatherer going about his business.

I followed a path round the bushes, towards the back

of the dense wood, forcing myself to walk as if I had all the time in the world. But my skin prickled at the thought that I was in the sight of a ruthless killer.

At last I reached the other side of the copse. I left the basket on the path and slipped between the trees. I couldn't see Delgado from here but I'd noted the trunk of the tree where he was hiding. I crept towards it, wincing at each twig crack. Every nerve in my body screamed at me to hurry but I resisted. I had to move quietly.

The crowd roared again. King Henry must have begun his contest. I hoped he wouldn't hit his opponent on the first run. *Please joust badly today, Sire*, I prayed. *Don't win until I've reached Delgado.*

I stopped underneath the tall fir. If I tried to climb it, it would shake and alert Delgado. I decided to take the beech growing next to it. The branches of the two trees intertwined. I'd be able to move towards him from there and hope he didn't see me. Surprise was on my side. I swung myself onto the lowest branch and began to pull myself up – slowly so as to make no noise. It wasn't long before I spotted the Spaniard. He was crouched on a high bough, watching the joust intently. The rising shouts of the crowd reached me as I eased myself up towards him.

I was close now. Another couple of branches and I'd be level with him. I reached for a handhold and broke a twig with a sickening crack. Delgado's head whipped round. I shrank behind the trunk, trying to keep my breathing under control. My palms were sticky and sweat trickled down my neck.

A triumphant fanfare alerted the marksman. He turned back to focus on his prey. I was high enough to see into the tiltyard now. The joust was over. With rising dread I saw the King climb up to the victor's platform.

I pulled myself level with Señor Delgado. The man was tense, intent on his target. Legs gripping the branch below, he carefully placed an arrow in his bow. Down in the tiltyard the crowd roared and the King blew kisses to Lady Anne. Then he put his hands to his head and raised his helmet high. I heard the creak of the yew wood as the bow was stretched.

'Delgado!' I shouted. 'Stop!'

The archer whipped round, the tension on the bow loosened for the moment. He saw me and a look of astonishment flickered across his face.

Then, with a cold intensity, he focused on the King once more and drew back the bowstring.

I threw myself at him, feeling the sting of branches whipping against my skin. As I crashed into him the archer sent his arrow speeding towards its target, the sound of its flight deafening in my ears. After a heartbeat, a terrible wail rose from the crowd and I knew the arrow must have found its mark. The King was dead.

34

I tried not to think about how I'd failed to protect King Henry. My job now was to make sure his assassin didn't get away. He was going to pay for his crime. But that wasn't going to be easy. Delgado grasped me by the neck. We sprawled on the branch and it juddered alarmingly under our weight. His grip tightened and I saw black spots before my eyes. I was losing consciousness.

I slumped against Delgado as if I'd fainted. It worked. The strangling grip loosened. At once I jabbed my bony elbows hard into the Spaniard's ribs. Delgado grunted in pain and let go. I struggled to face him but he punched me hard on the shoulder. Pain ripped through me and I began to slip from the branch. I flailed my arms, smashing my fingers against the trunk, the rough bark ripping my skin.

I made a desperate grab for Delgado's leather boot

and found myself swinging from his leg. I clung on with all my strength, feet scrabbling for a foothold. But there wasn't one.

Delgado cursed at me in Spanish and tried to shake me off. The next second a blade flashed down towards me. The man had a dagger! I twisted away but as the blade slashed close to my ear I lost my grip. I fell – but only a little way. By some miracle, I landed on a branch just below. I could still reach Delgado's boot. I gave it a sudden wrench. With a cry of fear, the Spaniard dropped his knife, flung out his arms to save himself and crashed through the sharp pine needles like a helpless rag doll.

He lay unmoving on the ground. He looked dead.

Fair punishment, I thought bitterly. But as I watched, he stirred, dragged himself to his feet, stood swaying for an instant, then limped off, scratched and blood-stained. I swung down through the branches after him.

Every bone in my body hurt as if I'd been run over by a cart – no, *fifteen* carts – but the King's murderer was not going to escape.

I heard the thundering of hooves and angry shouts. As I reached the last tree a band of Gentlemen of the Spears came galloping up. They must have worked out where the arrow had been fired from. I shrank against the trunk. If they saw me here they'd think I was the archer. As the horsemen thundered up, one gave a shout.

'There's the villain!'

I saw they were wheeling round and charging off. Delgado was stumbling ahead of them across the grounds as if he was the fox and they were the huntsmen. The guards had soon encircled him, the points of their spears at his throat.

They dragged him, whimpering, to the tiltyard. I crept along behind. Cries and screams rose from the other side of the wall. Part of me wanted to run far from the place, but I knew where my duty lay. If I didn't tell what I knew, the conspirators would get away with this horrific assassination.

Courtiers were surging around the yard in confusion and the yeomen were busy trying to calm them. This time there was no one to stop me slipping through the open gates. I saw my master straight away. He stood on the victor's platform. A motionless body lay at his feet, covered by a cloak. A pool of dark blood was trickling over the edge of the wooden boards. It was as I had feared – my King was dead. I felt sick to my stomach.

Under the velvet canopy guards had formed a barrier around the royal seats, halberds raised. In the centre sat Lady Anne, pale and distressed. Someone beside her was holding her hand, comforting her. I couldn't see who it was, but I felt flames of anger. Sir Ralph Lutterall had been in that chair earlier and so I was certain it was him whispering false words of sorrow into her ear.

I pushed past a woman wringing her hands and now

saw that the man with Lady Anne was not Sir Ralph. This man wore silver armour and he was tall with short cropped red hair. Was I dreaming? But no, there was no mistaking that giant of a man. It was King Henry himself!

Joy flooded through my body. My desperate lunge had spoilt the archer's aim after all. I'd saved the King's life!

But straight away my elation died. Delgado had still killed some poor unfortunate. Who was the victim? A hat lay next to the body – a bright blue velvet hat with a long peacock feather. I remembered who'd worn that garish adornment. It was Sir Ralph Lutterall lying dead on the ground, pierced by the arrow meant for the King. He must have joined the King on the platform so that his shock and distress would be seen by all after the fatal shooting.

He'd been justly punished by his own plot.

Trumpets sounded and at last the crowd fell silent.

'Bring the assassin forward!' ordered Cromwell.

Two yeomen dragged Delgado right past where I stood. He struggled against his captors, shouting out in Spanish. He looked pale with fright.

I searched the nearby faces for Harrington and Westbury. I may have deflected the archer's aim but the danger was not yet over. While those two remained free, the King was not safe. For all I knew, they'd already hatched another desperate plan.

A murmur started up in the crowd about Spanish

invasions. A woman fainted and the courtiers around her drew back, forcing me further from the platform. I started to push through towards my master, but I came up against a courtier who was stout and as hard to shift as an oak tree. I couldn't see anything now. But I could hear Delgado's fearful voice. He'd switched to English.

'I was paid to do it! Spare me and I will tell . . .'

A thrill of excitement jolted through me. The instant the names of the traitors fell from Delgado's lips, they'd be brought to justice. But suddenly there was a violent jostling in the crowd. John Westbury bounded up the steps of the platform and plunged his dagger into Delgado's heart.

35

The Spaniard slumped lifeless between his captors, his head lolling.

'There dies the assassin and good riddance to him!' declared Westbury. 'The foul murderer has killed Sir Ralph, a loyal Englishman.' Westbury cleaned his knife on Delgado's jerkin and held it up for everyone to see. There was a tremendous shout of approval from the crowd.

Delgado had been silenced. Now the only testimony to the plot was the letter in my jerkin.

'Let me through!' I cried. 'I must speak to Master Cromwell!'

But no one listened. They were too intent on the scene in front of them. The stout man shoved me aside and I almost fell.

'You were too hasty, sir,' Cromwell was telling Westbury. 'I would have questioned him before he was given his just punishment. I would have known who paid him.'

'Forgive me my fervour,' said Westbury earnestly, throwing down his knife. 'My heart led my actions.'

'And no one shall blame you,' came a commanding voice.

We all fell to our knees as the King came forward, flanked by his guard, three men deep.

I'd never get to Cromwell now. I thought of yelling to him above the crowd. But now as we rose to our feet again, everyone was calling out, 'God save His Majesty!' I had no chance of being heard.

The stout man shifted again, nearly crushing my toes. As I squirmed away in the press, I suddenly spotted Robert Aycliffe standing close by. I pushed through the throng, helped by my useful bony elbows and ignoring the angry curses as I passed. At last, Aycliffe was in reach. I tugged at his cloak.

He turned impatiently. He must have been wondering who was bothering him at such an important moment. His eyes flickered with something that looked like annoyance when he saw me.

'What do you want, boy?' he muttered, turning back to watch the King.

'Delgado's act was part of a conspiracy,' I whispered. 'Here's the proof.'

I thrust the letter into his hand.

As he read it, I saw him stiffen. He gave a brief nod, and held out the hilt of his sword, shoving aside the people in front of him. It was nearly as good as my bony elbows and earned him as many curses. However, everyone got out of his way and he quickly made a path towards Cromwell. The people in front of me moved together in his wake and I lost sight of him. I had no idea if the letter had reached Cromwell until I heard his voice.

'Arrest John Westbury!' he ordered.

I found a chink in the throng and was just in time to see King Henry whirl round in surprise. 'Are you mazed, good Thomas?' he demanded.

Two yeomen seized Westbury.

'I don't understand,' he gasped, his face the picture of innocence. 'What have I done?'

'You have committed treason!' snapped Cromwell.

Westbury struggled, writhing in the iron grip of the guards to face his monarch. 'Sire, your esteemed servant is mistaken. I am a loyal subject.'

'Master Cromwell, we would hear what you have to say,' said the King, dangerously calm.

Cromwell held out the letter. 'The words written here tell all, my Liege.'

'It cannot be!' cried Westbury. All around must have thought he was denying the crime, but I wondered if he was actually crying out in shock at the sight of his letter.

'Do you accuse one of our most trusted ministers of lying?' thundered the King. 'Pray continue, Thomas.'

'The prisoner hatched a deadly plot to kill his

monarch!' said Cromwell. A gasp ran through the crowd and Lady Anne gave a cry of terror. 'And your host, who lies dead before us, was part of that plot. He invited Your Majesty to his home, not as a guest, but as a target – to be the victim of an archer's arrow. It is little wonder Westbury wanted the assassin dead, for dead men cannot talk.'

As Cromwell spoke, Henry's face grew red with fury. Westbury tried to swallow. I didn't doubt that the man was picturing the horrors of his punishment to come.

'How did you come by this letter?' asked King Henry.

Cromwell's eyes flashed over the crowd. For the briefest of moments they found mine. I felt my heart stop. Then Cromwell said smoothly, 'It was discovered here at Lutterall House. There is no doubt that it was written by Sir Ralph and foul murder was planned by him and Westbury.'

I looked around at all the appalled faces and my stomach gave a jerk of horror. Hugh Harrington stood not two paces from me, his face expressionless, showing no fear. *But why should it?* I thought. *His name is not in the letter. He thinks himself safe.*

'What do you have to say now, Westbury?' thundered the King.

'I beg for mercy, my Liege.' The man's words came out in a croak. 'I was no willing participant. I have the names of those who . . . forced me to help them.'

'Good,' said the King coldly. 'Let us hope you do

not need help remembering them when you get to the Tower. Take him away!'

Everyone knew of King Henry's persuaders and their tools of the trade at the Tower of London. I glanced back towards Hugh Harrington to see what the effect of these words would be.

But the man had gone! Of course! Why would he stay to hear Westbury name him as a traitor? I barged my way towards the gates of the tiltyard, hoping I wasn't too late to find him.

Harrington was running towards the King's horse, which was tethered outside the walls, still armoured and sweating from the joust. I guessed his groom had gone into the tiltyard to watch the grim show.

Harrington released the horse's rope tether with a quick tug. He had one foot in the stirrup, but before he could spring into the saddle I leapt forward and clung to his back. We fell to the ground and the King's horse gave a whinny of fear and bolted.

Harrington threw me off, turned and raised his fist to strike. But suddenly he paused, a strange, puzzled look on his face. I decided to help him out. For a brief moment I shrivelled into Simkins and enjoyed Harrington's utter shock as he recognised the crookback thief.

'No, it can't be you!'

I jumped to my feet.

'You thought I'd drowned. Well, I'm no ghost and I'm not going to let you get away!' I cried.

I saw a flicker of fear in Harrington's eyes. Then the cold mask was back.

'You won't be doing anything!' he snapped.

He was holding something in his hand.

It was a gleaming metal tube with levers and an ornate handle. I'd never seen anything like it before, but I'd heard stories about such things, even in the abbey, and I knew only too well what it was. I'd always wanted to see one. It was my bad luck that my first sight of a pistol should be looking down its barrel. A bullet from a pistol could kill – and Harrington was about to pull the trigger.

36

I felt as if time had frozen. The blood thumped in my ears.

A horse flashed into view, galloping straight at us. It seemed to come from nowhere. The hooded rider was bent over the horse's neck, reins in one hand and a whip in the other. I threw myself to the ground. The horse passed so close I felt the beat of its hooves. Harrington ran for his life. He didn't get far. The horse was soon alongside him. The rider leant down, the whip lashed out and Harrington fell, his gun flying from his hand. His head hit the hard ground with a sickening crack.

I watched the horse gallop away and disappear among the trees.

Harrington was getting slowly to his knees, clutching his bleeding head. He began to crawl towards the fallen gun but, before his fingers got a grip on the weapon, I ran at him like a charging bull. Harrington gave a weak groan and collapsed. I sat firmly on his back.

'Seize him!' came a shouted order.

A sea of halberds was suddenly pointing straight at me.

'You don't understand . . .' I began. How was I going to explain why I'd floored one of the King's courtiers?

But the guards ignored me. They took Harrington roughly by the arms and pulled him to his feet.

'Shut your mouth, Jack, before you catch a fly in it,' said a familiar voice. It was Nicholas Mountford, and he was smiling. 'You've done a great deed. You caught the traitor! Westbury blabbed Harrington's name to the King and, the minute we get the order to make the arrest, we find you've done our work for us!' He picked up Harrington's pistol and held it at arm's length as if it was a snake. 'And the man was armed!'

'Well, it wasn't really me,' I began. 'Someone on horseback got him with his whip first. It was easy after that.'

Mountford looked puzzled.

'The rider on the big black horse,' I insisted. 'Didn't you see them?'

'No, lad,' said Nicholas Mountford. 'But we'd better find that rider. The King will want to thank him too. Where did he go?'

I was about to point to the woods, when I stopped myself just in time; I'd had a sudden suspicion who my rescuer was. I shrugged. 'I don't know. Maybe I imagined it.'

Mountford patted me on the head. 'Your pate's addled,' he laughed as he returned to join his men.

I slipped away through the gathering crowd and ran for the woods. I hadn't seen the face of the rider, but there had been something very familiar about that black horse. I plunged among the trees. Sure enough, Cat Thimblebee was standing next to Diablo, stroking his foaming neck.

'You saved my life!' I gasped. 'A few seconds later and I'd have been dead. How did you know I was in danger?'

'Mumble turned up at Whitehall,' said Cat, a wicked gleam in her eyes. 'I knew you wouldn't stay in the saddle all the way. Was it the ditch? You look dirty enough. Did I win my bet?'

Before I could tell her she hadn't, she went on. 'Anyway, I sent a message to Mister Wiltshire that I'd been summoned to Lutterall House as Lady Trevise had torn her favourite gown – and he knows that her ladyship will only let me do her mending – but instead, I got Diablo and came here. I could see you were in a bit of trouble and thought I'd lend a hand. Was that Harrington pointing the gun at you?'

I nodded. 'Thanks to you, the guards have got him. But what will happen if your master finds out you weren't really on an errand?'

'Lady Trevise is always having mishaps with her

linen and won't know any different if Mister Wiltshire should ask,' said Cat. She gave a delighted laugh. 'I knew you wouldn't manage without me! But I can't stand here gossiping! I've got you out of trouble – now I must go.' She swung herself up into the saddle and gathered the reins. 'See you back at Court.'

'Wait,' I said.

Cat pretended to sigh. 'What is it now?'

'Can you take me back to Whitehall? I don't want to face everyone yet. Nicholas Mountford will already be telling everyone how I captured Harrington singlehandedly . . .'

'Singlehandedly!' spluttered Cat, outraged.

'I know it's not true,' I said, 'but I can hardly say that you charged up and felled Harrington – on the King's horse. I'll just have to take the credit.'

Cat sniffed. 'I suppose so,' she said. 'Though it doesn't seem fair.'

'But I'll know,' I said seriously. 'And I really am grateful.'

Cat reached out a hand. 'Come on, then! You can have a ride, as long as you tell me what happened as we go.'

I clasped her tightly round her waist. 'I will if I can stay awake!' I said.

'We'll take it easy,' said Cat, grinning mischievously over her shoulder. 'I don't want to tire my darling Diablo.'

37

I made my way to the scribes' room. It was past noon, so I was hours late for work. Amazingly, I'd managed some sleep. The swaying motion of Diablo's walk had been too much for me and I'd suddenly woken, my head resting on Cat's shoulder as we neared the palace. The wretched girl had laughed like a drain and said I'd snored fit to scare the poor horse!

What was I going to say to Mister Scrope? Even if I could tell him the truth, the moment I said I'd been tied up and thrown into the Thames, had a fight in a tree and saved the King's life, the Chief Scribe would think I was mad. He'd send me to the Priory of St Mary of Bethlehem to be thrown in with all the other insane patients.

I ran through the empty passageways. Soon they'd be buzzing with the news of the traitors. But for now it was only Cat and me who knew the truth.

Lucky Cat! She'd been clever and had Mister Wiltshire's blessing for leaving the palace. I was going to be in trouble. I paused at the door and looked down at my livery. It was ripped and dirty and my hands were scraped raw from my fight in the tree. Luckily my other bruises were all hidden.

I took a deep breath, opened the door and went inside. Mister Scrope eyed me incredulously and Oswyn sneered. I wished Mark was there. It would have been nice to see a friendly face.

Oswyn Drage strolled over to me. 'The abbey boy's finally decided to join us.' He picked at a long tear in my red jacket, and a grin of evil delight spread over his face. 'What happened?'

I thought about all I'd gone through and I decided I'd had enough of Oswyn Drage.

'I came upon a bunch of villains,' I snarled, cracking my knuckles and making him jump. 'I beat them all. Do you have a problem with that?'

I stepped right up to him, eyeball to eyeball. Oswyn went pale and shook his head. He went back to his chair and began writing furiously.

'Enough of these tales,' growled the Chief Scribe. 'Why *are* you so late?'

'I was . . .' I began. But nothing came. I had no excuse for turning up so late. I looked again at Mark's empty chair. He might have made an excuse for me. And then inspiration struck.

'I am so sorry, Mister Scrope,' I said quickly. 'I was

207

called upon last night to deliver a message to Lutterall House and I forgot to leave you a note . . .' I hoped I could speak to Cromwell before Mr Scrope did!

'Hmm,' huffed Scrope. 'Well, you'll be paying for the mending of your jacket. Go and get it done now. You're a disgrace to your royal livery.'

My appearance at the sewing rooms caused a commotion.

'God's oath, boy, what have you been up to?' said Cat, giving me a secret wink. 'Hand me that jacket at once!'

But before I could, a messenger appeared at the door. 'Jack Briars here?' I nodded. 'The Sergeant Porter wants you at the Northern Gate. You have visitors.'

Puzzled, I walked after him down the passageway.

'Wait for me!' Cat was scuttling along behind, a skein of red cotton in her hand. 'I'm not being left out.'

A figure in a monk's habit was standing at the gate.

'Brother Matthew!' I cried. My godfather came towards me, smiling. But his face fell as he noticed my torn livery.

'I'm fine,' I assured him. 'Just a little accident.'

Then I spotted another figure, portly and squat, sitting on a donkey by the gate.

'Father Busbrig insisted we should visit you,' whispered Brother Matthew. 'He has brought gifts for your master but, if I were being unkind, I would suspect his motives.'

'Jack, my boy,' called the abbot in his oiliest voice.

'See, I have bottles of mead for Master Cromwell. Give them to me, Matthew.'

'Thank you, Father,' I said. 'I'll take them.'

'You will not,' said the abbot, snatching the basket. 'I insist on giving them to him myself.'

'I'm afraid you will have a long wait,' I replied, trying to keep a straight face. 'Master Cromwell is not at Court.'

A distant sound of trumpets reached us. 'Make way!' ordered the Sergeant Porter. 'Make way for His Majesty! Move that mangy animal.'

'I'll help!' offered Cat. Before Father Busbrig could heave himself off the donkey, she took the rope bridle and led it away, the bottles of mead chinking merrily in their basket.

'Stop!' shrieked the abbot helplessly, as Cat slapped the donkey on the rear to hurry it up. 'I want to meet the King.'

His cries were lost in the thunder of hoofbeats and sound of trumpets. The King had arrived.

38

Everyone drew back for the royal procession. Thomas Cromwell was riding just behind King Henry. They were flanked by the Gentlemen of the Spears. We all bowed deeply as the King approached.

'Stop!' boomed His Majesty. 'There is someone here I would speak with.'

I looked up. To my astonishment the King was staring down at me.

'Jack Briars, is it not?' he said. 'The boy with the flying pies.'

'Yes, my Liege,' I murmured, my heart thumping.

'Nicholas Mountford tells me you are to be congratulated,' the King went on. 'He says that you acted most speedily in capturing the scoundrel, Harrington.'

'I am Your Majesty's servant,' I said humbly.

King Henry looked me up and down. 'A rather

battered-looking servant at the moment, young man,' he said. 'Your livery needs repair.'

Cat came forward, held up her red cotton and bobbed a curtsey. 'Cat Thimblebee, Your Grace. I work for Mister Wiltshire, Your Grace. If it please Your Grace, that is all in hand, Your Grace.'

'Excellent!' said the King. 'You may tell Mister Wiltshire to send the repair bill to the royal purse.'

'Yes, Your Grace,' said Cat, backing away and curtseying all the while. 'Thank you, Your Grace.' She suddenly broke into a run. The abbot had managed to turn the donkey round and was heading our way. Cat shooed him off. The donkey brayed in alarm and broke into a gallop, heading for St James's Park. The abbot's wails became fainter.

I made sure I kept my face straight in front of my monarch, but it wasn't easy.

'You work for Master Cromwell,' said the King, 'when you are not juggling pastries?'

'Yes, Sire,' I answered. 'I am one of his scribes.'

The King bent towards me so that only I caught his next words. 'And more than that, or so I've heard.' Was the King telling me that he knew about my extra tasks – the secret ones? I felt a thrill of excitement.

He straightened and turned to Cromwell. 'You have a good lad here, Thomas. I'm sure you will use *all* of his talents.'

'Aye, Your Majesty,' said Cromwell, bringing his horse alongside. 'I am ever thankful for Jack's loyalty.'

King Henry nodded and looked up at the white walls of his palace. 'It pleases us to be back safely,' he said, urging his horse forward.

The procession moved on. Cromwell waited for them to pass and then dismounted.

'You went beyond your brief, Jack,' he said sternly.

I gulped. 'I'm sorry . . .' I began, trembling in case his next words were my dismissal.

'In future you will follow orders,' he said, 'but this time it was well that you didn't. You persevered when no one else recognised the danger. I'm impatient to hear how you uncovered this deadly plot entirely alone.'

Little did he know of the vital help I'd had from my friends. I was thankful Cat couldn't hear my master's words – she'd be outraged that she wasn't able to take any of the credit. And I was even more thankful that Mark knew nothing of his part – he'd faint away on the spot!

'You have justified my belief in you, Jack,' Cromwell went on. 'You will be valuable to me, I am certain of it.'

No dismissal – and even a hint of more missions to come!

'There is someone here I wish to meet,' said Cromwell, looking over my shoulder to where my godfather stood humbly waiting.

Brother Matthew shuffled awkwardly forwards.

'Jack is a credit to you,' Cromwell told him. 'He's most valuable to our office.'

'I've no doubt of it, sir,' said Brother Matthew proudly. 'He's always been a quick-witted lad, despite his humble beginnings.'

'He and I are cut from the same cloth,' said Cromwell. 'Who knows where his skills may take him?'

Cat suddenly appeared at my elbow. 'And once he's learnt to ride, sir, they can take him even further.'

Cromwell raised an eyebrow.

'Not learning, sir,' I said quickly. 'I'm ... just improving my technique. My teacher is very good.'

'Can't say the same about the pupil,' muttered Cat.

God's teeth! She'd got the last word again!